LETTERS OF A CIVIC GUARD

LETTERS OF A CIVIC GUARD

John B. Keane

THE MERCIER PRESS
Dublin & Cork

The Mercier Press
4 Bridge Street, Cork
25 Lower Abbey Street, Dublin 1.

ISBN 0 85342 463 2

INTRODUCTION

Leo Molair, chief author of the following letters, is a member of the Garda Siochana, that most repected and distinguished of peace-keeping forces which has almost always succeeded in attracting to its ranks a most superior and dedicated type of individual.

Leo Molair is a man of honour but he is also possessed of a wry and somewhat caustic sense of humour. For reasons best known to himself he never took a wife although it could be said that as years went by he became married to his vocation.

The preservation of peace always was and is his primary function but because the strict enforcement of the code does not always succeed in maintaining order he is often obliged to harness the chariot of the law to the horses of discretion and humanity.

He is the man on the spot and as such knows the value of such effective weapons as tact and delicacy. He also knows the case histories of his clients the way a family doctor knows his patients.

He is always mindful of the evil of wrongdoing but mindful too of many areas of innocence relating thereto and it is here that discretion and insight of a high order are needed if the law is to serve rather than expose the community.

If some of these letters read seamily or sordidly it is not the fault of the author. Rather it is the fault of the community which has been entrusted to his care. If there were not a seamy side to life there would be no necessity for custodians of the peace. Leo Molair's role is one which has been created by the follies and weaknesses of his fellows.

5

Consequently folly and weakness must, perforce, dominate the greater part of the following correspondence.

We find our man, towards the end of his career, writing to his nephew Ned who is also a civic guard but of a mere two years standing.

*   *   *

Garda Barracks,
Monasterbawn,
Co. Cork.

Dear Ned:

You ask about your new Super. I had a visit four years ago from the same Patcheen Conners who now answers to the call of Superintendant Patrick Conners. We were together in the Depot and afterwards we spent a spell in the same station in Dublin. Patcheen has an accent now like you'd hear from an elocution teacher. On top of that he needlessly indulges in a lot of other grandiose antics. The wife, of course, must shoulder the blame.

Answering to the name of Susie McGee she graduated thirty years ago from a juicy ranch of nine acres in the latter end of Mayo and between cajoling and screeching, nagging and pestering you might say she would be entitled to take full credit for all of Patcheen's promotions. Fair dues to her she was and still is a fine ball of a woman. There are some unkind souls who say she went to bed a half a dozen times with a certain politician, once for sergeant, twice for inspector and three times for superintendent. However, you may take it from me that those who spread such stories come under the general head of hostile witnesses.

Patcheen was alright when I first knew him. He was as easy-going as an in-calf heifer, tough as an ass, fond of a pint and afraid of nothing of God's earth until he was hooked and gaffed by the aforementioned Susie McGee.

6

She was the oldest of seven sisters and neighbours who knew them will give evidence that not one of them drew on a knickers till the day they went into service.

Susie came to Dublin to work as a housemaid for a surgeon named Halligan. She was only barely gone eighteen at the time. She arrived in the city in the middle of March and she married Patcheen Conners in the middle of June. She changed him overnight.

About six months after the marriage I called to see them one evening when I was off-duty. They had their own house in a nice area of Rathmines.

There was Patcheen, made up by the wife like he'd be a magazine model with cardigan and slippers and a fart of a pipe hanging from the side of his mouth. We sat down for a chat. From the minute I took to the chair he never stopped sermonising about the evils of drink and the terrible after-effects of late-night carousing. After a while Susie landed in with three small cups and a tiny teapot you wouldn't put in front of a midget.

There was no mention of drink and I having a head on me like a furnace after a party the night before. After a while Susie says to me:

'How's your handicap?'

I told her it was as good as could be expected thinking she was referring to my private part. I was ruptured earlier in the year making an arrest outside a public house in Henry Street.

'Patrick's,' said she, 'is down to fourteen.'

'Twas then I knew she must be referring to golf. I nearly fell out of the chair because when I first met Patcheen he wouldn't know a golf club from a hockey stick. Susie is one of those strong-willed women who will never latch on to a made man. They prefer to start with their own raw material, no matter how rugged or crude, and to mould what they want out of that. The husbands have no say whatsoever in the outcome. She did a fair job on Patcheen. When I knew him he wouldn't track an elephant through six inches of snow. Anyone who could make a superintendent out of Patcheen Conners could make a bonfire out of snowballs. He called here once to see me. He didn't stay with me long. He had an appointment for a four-ball at Muskerry Golf Club. Susie stayed in the car so I came out to say hello to her. You'd hardly expect a woman so high-up in the world to call into a one-man station.

'You'll never marry now,' was the first thing she said to me.

'Not unless you divorce Patcheen,' said I by way of a joke.

'Surely you mean Pawtrick,' she said and she cocked her nose high.

'He'll always be Patcheen to me, missus,' said I.

That stung her. What the poor woman keeps forgetting is that the only real difference between myself and Patcheen Conners is the colour of our uniforms. Patcheen himself is alright. You don't have to worry about him. All he wants is to draw his pay, play golf and be seen in his uniform now and again. My fondest regards to Gert and the baby. Find out the names for me of the older guards and sergeants in your division. Chances are I know some of them.

·Your fond uncle,
Leo.

Main Street,
Monasterbawn,
Co. Cork.

Dear Guard Molair:

Sacred heart of Jesus and his divine Mother will you do something about the carry-on at Fie's public house. I am the mother of a family that never put a hard word on no one but the conduct going on here you wouldn't hear of in Soho. At all hours of the morning is the after-hours guzzling of drink going on, single men hobnobbing with married

8

women and vice versa if you please. God alone knows what amount of whoring goes on there. If you don't do your duty and close down this den of iniquity before the whole village is corrupted and scandalised I will write to the minister that you are turning a blind eye on criminal and immoral activity. Margie Fie is worse nor any madam you'd find in a whorehouse with her lips daubed scarlet and the make-up an inch thick and the grey hair dyed blonde. Who does she think she's codding. Hurry up quick and close her down in the name of all that's good and holy.

> Devoted Catholic wife
> and mother of a large family.

> Main Street,
> Monasterbawn.

Dear Guard Molair:

It is high time someone took the initiative in the stamping out of after-hours drinking and other vices that arise from it. Wives are without money for their shopping and many children in this God-forsaken village are hungry and without proper clothing. The money is squandered on drink to buy style for the wives of certain publicans. The most brazen example of after-hours boozing is to be seen at Crutt's public house right here under your very nose in Monasterbawn. On my way from eight o'clock Mass yesterday morning what did I behold outside the front door of Crutt's pub but a rubber object which I took at first to be a finger-stall or some sort of unblown balloon. Casually over breakfast I described the object to my husband. Imagine my horror when he told me that what I had seen was undoubtedly a contraceptive. Hell is a light punishment for the proprietors of Crutt's public house.

> Signed,
> Indignant Housewife.

9

Dear Uncle Leo:

Many thanks for your letter and for the enclosed gift of which there was no need as we have more than enough. We are all very distraught and upset here after the brutal murder of our colleague yesterday. It is incredible that an Irishman should gun down another Irishman in cold blood merely because the victim was doing his duty and upholding the law for the benefit of all the citizens of the state. There is a despairing feeling of futility at the callousness of these extremists who snuff out life without thought for loved ones left behind. I cannot conceive of a more foul and brutal deed. Those who murdered this likeable and loyal member of our force cannot be called men. Yet the arch-criminals who are their superiors walk the streets as free men with smug looks on their faces. God forgive me if I ask Him to wipe these scum from the face of the earth. I'll say no more now as I may say too much. I see the gentle smile on my dead comrade's face and I hear his light laugh fading away forever. It's terrible.

I envy you your peaceful way of life down there, far from the madding crowd and all that and the clean country-side at your doorstep. It is my ambition to move down the country as soon as possible. I'm checking up on the older members of the division to find out who would have been most likely to have served with you. I'll write as soon as I hear from you again. Be thankful for the grand, quiet, peaceful place where you live and for the innocent people in your bailiwick.

Your fond nephew,
Ned.

P.S. We are making a collection for the widow.

Ned.

Dear Ned:

I enclose a subscription towards the collection for our dead comrade's widow. A horrible business altogether. How should one react when one's brother is murdered, gunned down mercilessly without a chance of any kind and remember that we who wear these uniforms are brothers and comrades in the cause of law and order. All we must endeavour to do is protect our charges, the small boys and girls, the fathers and the mothers, the senile and the helpless and to see to the safety of their belongings and their homes. Nothing must come between us and our concern for those in our care. If one of us is brutally murdered by so-called republicans our function is to stand fast and to pray for the resolution and courage to carry on with the job. We may ask ourselves how any human being could cut down another in his prime without regard for his young wife and family. We may ask ourselves how such an awful deed can be justified. We may ask if there is any form of punishment on this earth severe enough for these inhuman wretches who spill our life's blood. We may ask and ask Ned but in the end all that matters is the honourable discharge of our duty regardless of all other considerations and this force, in that respect, can look to its record with pride.

Like yourself I will draw the line here and now on this most tragic event. Stick to your post. Be loyal to your superiors and to your comrades and there need be no fears for the future of our country.

In your letter you say to me that I should be thankful for this grand, quiet, peaceful place where I live and also for the innocent people in my bailiwick. Wait till you're as old as I am and you'll find out that there aren't as many innocent people as you think. There is an extract from Hamlet which goes like this:

I could a tale unfold, whose lightest word

Would harrow up thy soul; freeze thy young blood;
Make thy two eyes, like stars, start from their spheres;
Thy knotted and combined locks to part,
And each particular hair to stand on end,
Like quills upon the fretful porpentine
But this eternal blazon must not be
To ears of flesh and blood.

I too my dear Ned could a tale unfold, in fact a hundred tales, about this village and no other, that would make the *News of the World* read like a Communion tract but this would achieve no worthwhile end except to do the world of harm and absolutely no good.

If you think Monasterbawn is quiet and peaceful read this account of one particular day in the life of your humble servant, Leo Molair. I rose at seven-thirty and went to eight o'clock Mass which I had to serve for the good reason that the altar boy's mother forgot to call him. How could she and she at a wren dance till five in the morning. On my way from Mass I was summoned to a house in Jackass Lane by a gorsoon of eight who informed me that his father was in the process of murdering his mother. From the casual way he spoke I gathered it wasn't his first time murdering her. I arrived at the house to find the poor woman seated on a chair with a bleeding mouth, a swollen right eye and a cut nose. The husband whose name is Mocky Trembles was still giving out when I crossed the threshold. My first instinct was to lay him out but when you're in this game as long as I am you'll find it pays to play cool. I started attempts at reconciliation at quarter to nine and six cups of tea later at precisely eleven o'clock I had the two of them cooing like pigeons and Mocky promising never to lay a finger on her ever again. For her part she knelt and swore that not a nagging word would be heard out of her as long as she lived.

When I left he was bathing her face with a sponge and telling her that she was to keep the next allotment of family allowance money in order to buy some style for herself. Mocky drank the last allotment.

12

Back at the barracks there was a caller awaiting me. She was the female teacher in the national school down the road, a spinster by the name of Monica Flynn who, if I may say so, has had strong matrimonial designs on yours truly although if you saw her you wouldn't give me any credit. Monica had arrived to make a complaint about a man called the Bugger Moran. She had some difficulty in explaining herself but I gathered that the Bugger had been exposing his population stick, if you'll pardon the expression, opposite the young girls on their way home from school. I promised to look into the matter. Monica refused to proffer charges for fear of embarrassing herself, the school and the children. Rest assured that the Bugger will have a sore posterior shortly.

When Monica departed I had my breakfast and took a skim through the paper. My next chore was to visit the farm of a man called Thade Buckley about five miles up in the mountains. No hope of a lift in that direction so late in the day with all the creamery cars long gone. Nothing for it but the bicycle. I arrived after nearly an hour on the uphill road. Some months previously at a bull inspection the same Thade had a yearling rejected and it was my job to ensure that certain requirements be fulfilled if he was to keep the animal.

'What brought you?' asked Thade with an innocent face and he knowing well what brought me.

'You had a bull for inspection lately?'

'I had a bull,' said Thade.

'And did you castrate that bull,' I asked, 'in compliance with the departmental order?'

'I squeezed that bull myself,' said Thade, 'and you may be sure that he is now a happy bullock grazing the mountain.'

'He must be a very odd sort of a bullock,' said I, 'seeing that he attacked and nearly killed a fowler last Sunday.'

'That's the first I heard of it,' said Thade. I then instructed him to locate the bull for me so he led me across a few wet fields to the base of the mountain where sure enough there were some bullocks grazing. He pointed at the animal in question. I noted that this beast was castrated beyond doubt but when I looked for the rejection mark on his ear which the departmental inspector impresses on all rejects I could find no trace of it. Alongside this animal was another with a wicked-looking pair of bloodshot eyes and he pawing the ground indicating a charge at any minute. Sure enough in his ear was the letter 'R'. The animal was not castrated it was plain to be seen.

'Explain this,' I asked Thade but when I turned he was haring his way down the mountain. The next thing you know I got an almighty thump on the rump and there was the rejected bull coming at me again. I followed Thade's example and scrambled over a gate into a nearby field. Back at the house I confronted Thade.

'I must have squeezed the wrong one,' he explained, 'or else they must have grown there again.' I had enough of this nonsense. I charged him with possession of a reject and refused his offer of whiskey which I strongly suspected was home-made anyway. Three years earlier his house had been searched from top to bottom for poitcheen but not a drop was found. I discovered later from a friend that under every bed in the house was an enamel chamber pot and every one of these pots was filled to the brim with a liquid which was not urine.

When I arrived back at the barracks it was too late for lunch although there is always a plate kept hot for me at the house where I normally have lunch. There were two visitors awaiting me at the barracks. One was an elderly woman who had just been badly bitten by a dog and the other an unfortunate woman whose husband had suddenly and mysteriously disappeared. I took particulars from both women and went into action. A phone call confirmed what I suspected about the missing man. He had spent the family allowance money the night before, in Clonakilty, started a row in a chip-shop and wound up in the barracks where he

14

was still being held for refusing to identify himself. The orderly promised to send him home in the patrol car some time that night. As for the cross dog the poor creature is now in the kennels of Heaven.

Three o'clock. The children would now be coming from school. I took up my position in a concealed entrance where I had a good view of the roadway. At three the school bell rang and at five past three our friend the Bugger appeared and pretended to be relieving himself. When the children appeared he exposed himself fully so I moved in and arrested him. I first of all gave him a good rooter in the behind. Then for good measure I let him have two more boosters in the same spot. Then I lugged him to the barracks where I charged him. His pleading not to charge him was piteous. The awful disgrace of it and the effect it would have on his mother, a doting old crone who would hardly know night from day.

I decided to let him go but I warned him if I ever caught him again I would personally belt the daylights out of him and see that he went to jail as well. It wasn't out of pity for him or his mother but the prospect of undesirable publicity for the whole village. At five Jerry Fogg the postman arrived with the morning post. We had an arrangement that if I was missing from the barracks he would hold the post until my return.

There were two letters, one each from the wives of two publicans who have premises at opposite sides of the street. They think I don't know who writes them. I know more about them than they know about themselves. Remember I have been studying these people night and day for twenty-five years, since I was transferred here from Mayo for raiding a public house. Both do good business and are fairly well off but the letters are motivated by jealousy. I dare not take a drink in either house for fear of invoking the enmity of the other. Whenever I feel like a few drinks I slip in the rear door of the Widow Hansel's pub at the northern end of the village. No one sees me come and no one sees me go.

15

Sometimes I have a game of thirty-one in the kitchen with Jerry the post and a few pals. I'll file the letters and ignore them.

Four-thirty. Time to take a stroll around the village and make sure that everything is alright. Five-thirty, back at the barracks. Boiled two eggs and made a pot of tea. Turned on the television and sat back to relax. Enter a small fat woman whose face is vaguely familiar. She is accompanied by a pimple-faced, teenage girl who looks sufficiently like her to be her daughter. She gets down to business right away.

'My child is after being raped,' she says.

'Will you state the particulars missus,' says I as calmly as I could.

'Well,' says she, 'she's in service below at Jamesy Cracken's these past four months and she hasn't had a minute's peace with the same Jamesy chasing her at every hand's turn. Finally he done it. This very evening he raped the child in the henhouse.'

I nodded, awaiting the remainder of the story.

'I don't see you taking no notes,' she said.

'Notes about what?' said I.

'About the rape,' said she.

'And was it you or your daughter was raped missus,' said I.

'My daughter,' said she. That quietened her awhile. I set about finding out what really happened to the daughter. Apparently, Jamesy Cracken, a feeble old lecher of seventy-four, attempted to knock the girl on the floor of the henhouse where she had been sent by Jamesy's sister to collect eggs for the supper. All, it transpired, that Jamesy succeeded in doing was thrusting his hand under her dress where it trespassed on that most prized and private of all personal properties. The innocent young girl, presuming this to be rape, ran home screeching to her mother who, with a nose for easy money, came first to the barracks before launching on a campaign to milk Jamesy Cracken of some of the thousands he is supposed to have hoarded over the years. I burst the bubble there and then and informed her that the only charge, to my knowledge, of which Jamesy might be guilty was indecent assault and that her best bet, in such a situation, would be an ambitious solicitor.

Do you still think that this is a quiet and peaceful place? Remember that, at the time of writing, it is only eight o'clock and that the ship of night has yet to discharge its mysterious cargo. I'm tired. It's been a long, long day. I think I'll slip up to the Widow Hansel's and chance a few pints.

> Love to Gert and the child.
> Uncle Leo.

> Fallon Street, G. S.
> Dublin 13.

Dear Uncle Leo:

Good to hear from you. I suppose I shouldn't complain. I have a nice home, a lovely wife and child and a good job. There are times when I am driven to despair. One night last week I interrupted a smash and grab raid in Grafton Street. There were two youths involved. As soon as they saw me they took off in different directions. I followed one and after a chase cornered him in a lane near the Shelbourne Hotel. He produced a knife but I managed to disarm him. What do you think happens? A suspended sentence of six months. The mother arrived at the court to plead for him. I risk my life to arrest him and instead of a jail sentence the judge gives him permission to further his career of crime. Would you blame me if I were to close my eyes the next time I come across a smash and grab?

There is an old guard here by the name of Mick Drea who says he was stationed with you in Mayo. He says he could write a book about the times the pair of you had together. Tell me about the raid on the pub and why it was the cause of your being transferred. Young Eddie is grand. Gert sends her love.

Your fond nephew,
Ned.

Main Street,
Monasterbawn.

Dear Guard Molair:

This is to acquaint you with a terrible disturbance that took place outside Crutt's public house just on midnight on the thirtieth of November while yourself and the Widow Hansel were cavorting and doing what else among the tombstones of Monasterbawn Graveyard. They all but kicked one another to death but who is to blame teenagers if they are given rotten whiskey by Mrs Crutt. They were no more than children the creatures. Well might their poor mothers curse the demon that took their money and threw them out drunk and incapable on the cold street. May the blessed Mother of God forgive her for I cannot. I am writing to Superintendent Fahy since it seems to be a waste of time writing to you.

Signed,
A devoted wife and Catholic
mother of a large family.

Garda Station,
Monasterbawn.

Dear Ned:

I can understand your frustration but the last thing any judge wants to be is first to jail a youngster. What that pup needed was a good hiding, a hiding he'd remember every time he'd see a guard but that's frowned upon now and these days in cities there's little fear and less respect for the uniform and you'll have less still while you have lenient courts and naive judges who play games with the law with their fines of ten and twenty pounds on young bucks who pay more than that on income tax every week. As far as I can see courts are presently no more than places where licenses to commit crimes are issued to snot-nosed whelps who should be flogged and isolated until they show respect for society. I'm all for giving a young fellow a chance but too many chances make a mockery of my job and yours.

I remember Mick Drea well. For many years he was my closest friend. We were stationed in Mayo together in those days when the sight of a guard's uniform enraged the local bucks. Their sole aim was to have it to their credit that they kicked or beat the stuffing out of a guard. Off then to England where they'd be boasting about their exploits in pubs and Irish clubs. Mick and myself were stationed in the tiny village of Keeldown. There were several pubs and several shebeens. Shebeens sprang up overnight. What happened was this. A young navvy would arrive home from England with maybe a hundred or more pounds. Mighty money in those days. In case he might spend it foolishly on drink for others the mother might advise him to invest it and what better way could you invest money than in drink. That was how many shebeens started. Most were quickly found out and closed when reports would be sent to the barracks by the proprietors of other shebeens whose trade had suffered a knock because of the new opposition. The stock of a shebeen consisted mainly of porter and poitcheen, a few bottles of the very cheapest in sherry and port wines and inevitably a wide range of the most inferior Spanish brandies. These were easily purchased at the nearest fishing port from the crews of trawlers operating out of San Sebastian and Bilbao in the north of Spain. Two shillings a bottle was the going rate and for this you got a pint and a quarter of a concoction powerful enough to fuel a spaceship to the moon. Quite often an overdose of it resulted in permanent mental and physical damage and, on occasion, death.

On very rare occasions there would be legitimate Hen-

19

nessy's brandy but this was almost always beyond the scope
of the regular patrons. Usually it was sold at four-pence a
thimbleful to old men and women and those who might be
invalided or convalescing. I was witness to several murderous
brawls which could be directly attributed to the consumption of a mixture of Spanish brandy and poitcheen. One
night in the height of summer Mick Drea and myself cycled
in plain clothes to a shebeen in the north of the county. It
was situated near a dancehall. In the kitchen there was one
long stool and six chairs all told. There was a table in the
centre. The bar was a tea chest on top of which was a biscuit
tin which was used as a till. Most of the customers were
seated on the floor drinking happily or crooning snatches of
songs, some in Gaelic, some in English. The hardest drinkers
would be the navvies home on holidays from England. They
sat, as I say, on the floor and when Mick and I entered they
eyed us with great suspicion and deliberately bumped or
fell against us when we made our way to the counter. Those
on the floor were drinking their shorts out of eggstands,
eggshells, stolen inkwells and saltcellars. They drank porter
out of cups, mugs and pannies. There was a brisk trade and
I wondered if the local guards knew about the place.
Unlikely since it was only a few weeks old. We called and
paid for two mugs of porter and surveyed the situation
without pretending to do so. After a while a dwarfish
fellow with a cap on the side of his head and a crooked
smile asked us where we came from. It was easy to see that
he was the spokesman for a group of young thugs who sat
drinking shorts in the nearest corner.

'Foxford,' we lied.

'And what line of trade does ye be in whilst ye're there?'
he asked.

'We're in the bank,' Mick told him.

'Are ye Mayo men itself?' he asked, turning to wink
knowingly at his cronies who had meanwhile edged a bit
nearer so that they could hear better.

'Indeed we're not,' said we.

20

'Musha you have the poll of a Galway man whatever,' he told Mick.

'He's from Cork,' said I.

'Musha we have nothing against Corkmen, eh boys,' he addressed his friends.

'Yourself. Where are you from?' he demanded. I was about to say Kerry but since he had declared that they had nothing against Corkmen I decided to opt for that county.

'I don't like one bit of this,' I whispered to Mick. 'Let's move out of here. I can smell trouble.' We finished our drinks and headed for the dancehall. It was crowded. Mick wasn't long in finding himself a partner. She was a beautiful dark-haired girl with a pale face. I took a few turns on the floor but could meet nothing I fancied. The next thing you know Mick comes across to me and announces that he is seeing the girl home. Kathleen is her name and she lives only a half mile up the road.

'You keep an eye on the bikes,' Mick said. 'I won't be gone long.' We arranged to meet at the crossroads below the village. I pushed the cycles in that direction and waited. It was a warm night without a puff of wind. The stars shone in their millions and the moon was full. There was a rich scent of honeysuckle and I thought how peaceful it all was. It was then I heard the footsteps. After a while I made out the shapes. I had no bother in recognising the dwarfish fellow with the slanted cap and undoubtedly the four with him would have to be the four who had been squatting on the floor of the shebeen although I couldn't swear to this. I sensed they were looking for me so I drew away from the roadway and crouched under a convenient whitethorn bush. The next thing I heard was 'Come out you effin Peeler, we know you're there.' I made no move. If only Mick would return, I thought, the two of us might be able for them. Someone in the shebeen must have recognised Mick or myself and spread the word. They were all shouting now. The language was obscene. I crossed myself and started to pray. It was as if I had invoked disaster because at that instant cadhrawns of black turf and fist-sized stones fell in a shower around me. One of the stones landed on my left shoulder and nearly paralysed me. I was forced into coming out but there were only three of them on the roadway. The small man and another seemed to have disappeared.

'What do you want?' I asked fearfully.

'Your effin blood,' said one.

'What harm did I ever do to any one of you?' I asked.

'You're an effin guard,' said the same man and he came for me swinging. I ducked and caught him smartly in the jaw. He went down without a sound. Two to go I thought. The odds have shortened. I braced myself for the other two but they seemed reluctant to mix it. I decided to make a run for it and try to intercept Mick on his way back. It was then I was struck from behind. I remember no more after that. When I came to I was in hospital. I had a fractured jaw, three smashed ribs and a cut on the forehead which required several stitches. I was black and blue all over and the doctor assured me that I was lucky to be alive. The gang had left me for dead for when Mick returned that was his first impression. My attackers went to England the follow-ing day. The shebeen was raided and the stock destroyed that night. I spent a fortnight in the hospital and another fortnight at home with my mother, God rest her soul. I went back on duty after that. The incident, terrible and all as it was, taught me one invaluable lesson A civic guard has to watch his every move. If, while off duty, his presence causes antagonism or resentment he should remove himself from the scene at once. It is unfair and unjust I know but the truth is the minute you don the uniform of the guards it's the same as if you pulled a jersey over your head. You are a member of the team of law and order for the rest of your life. You are irrevocably committed. In short, you're a marked man.

Mick went back to the place again the following Sunday night. He had fallen in love with his dark-haired Kathleen. For six successive months he paid her court and then unex-

22

pectedly, one Sunday night, she jilted him. He demanded a reason and at first she was reluctant to tell him. He insisted that he was entitled to know so she gave in. That very morning after Mass her father discovered that she was doing a line with a guard. He had overheard it in a pub. When he got home he summoned his daughter up to her bedroom and there he told her that she was never to have anything to do with a man wearing a uniform, no love, no friendship, no nothing be he priest, parson, peeler or trooper. He told her that he would blow her brains out if she did not send Mick Drea packing immediately. When Mick heard this he told her he would resign his position but still she refused.

'My Da do maintain,' said she, 'that once tainted is always tainted.'

Give Mick my best regards and my love to your care.

As ever,
Your fond uncle,
Leo.

District Headquarters.

Dear Leo:

I haven't time to call so you need not expect me for inspection this month. I am enclosing a number of letters received over the past few weeks from anonymous scribes in your quarter of the world. You'll have to do something about these public houses although I remember you telling me once that the wives of the proprietors are the authors of the letters. Nevertheless, you had better give them a reminder one of these Sunday nights. I'll leave the timing etcetera to your own discretion. Just let them know who is boss. One of the letters, as you will see, accuses you of indulging in black magic and other forms of witchcraft with Nance Hansel in Monasterbawn graveyard at the witching hour. Give Nance my regards by the way and tell her she is to stay with us whenever she comes to town.

You know me Leo. I don't believe a word about this graveyard business but like yourself I also have superiors who may question me about the goings-on in Monasterbawn. All it needs is one bitchy letter or an anonymous phone call to some newspaper and then we're all in trouble. Just let me know the score Leo. I must know about everything that happens in my district. Not alone must I know everything but I must be the first to know everything. I'll see you as soon as I can. If you have any problem that you cannot put down on paper or talk about over the phone drop in some night and we'll talk it over. That's what we're here for.

Sincerely,
Joe Fahy,
(Superintendent).

Jackass Lane,
Monasterbawn.

Dear Guard Molair:
Last week my husband gave me none of his wages and I had to tick the groceries. This happens often. He spends the money in Fie's pub where he goes to play darts every night. I haven't had a decent stitch of clothes in over five years only hand me downs my sister sends me from England. All he does is give out whenever I ask for money for the house. My children are often hungry. I'm sure if Fie's were closed at the normal time he would be alright as he does not go there till close on closing time. He is barred from Crutt's and the Widow's over he rising rows. God forbid I should get you into trouble Guard Molair as I know you are a decent man. The truth is if you did your duty there would be no after-hours drinking. I am going to have to write to the minister if you don't get a move on.

Signed,
Hungry Home.

Dear Ned:

Sorry for not writing sooner but I've been up to my eyes.
This can be a most complicated job at times with so many
awkward situations to resolve. Don't mention perjury to me.
I have had my bellyful of it over the years. Take note of the
following.

Last week I had Thade Buckley up for having seven un-
licensed dogs. I had warned him repeatedly but he chose to
ignore me. In the court he was asked by the clerk to take
the oath.

'Do you,' said the clerk, 'promise to tell the truth, the
whole truth and nothing but the truth?'

'I do,' said Thade in a loud voice and then in a whisper
he says, 'I do in my arse.' I heard him quite plainly from
where I was standing inside the door of the courthouse near
the dock. I requested the judge to make him take the oath
again. You must know by now Ned that judges have no
patience with guards who take up the time of the court. He
agreed to my request however. Thade was approached
secondly by the clerk who asked the appropriate question.

'I do,' he said in the same loud voice. Then in an almost
inaudible whisper, 'I do in my arse.' I knew from the look
on the judge's face that another request from me would be
turned down flatly. No blame to him. He couldn't be
expected to hear Thade's whispers from where he sat.
Thade swore on his oath that none of the dogs was his, that
they were owned by tinkers and horseblockers, while others
were strays. The case was dismissed. Perjury used to be a
reserved sin in Kerry until recently which means it was
common there but believe me it was almost as common
everywhere else. I remember that case in Kerry involving a
small farmer. His thirteen acres had grown over a year to
fourteen. This happened because he kept extending his
paling sticks into a neighbouring, boggy commonage. He
was reported by other users of the commonage. He was

asked by the clerk, 'Do you swear to tell the truth, the whole truth and nothing but the truth?'

'I do boy,' he said. 'Oh jaysus I do.' Then to himself he says, 'I do in my hole.'

'What's that?' asked the judge. 'What did you say?'

'I said, "'pon my soul my lord".'

'There is no need for the embellishments,' said the judge who addressed himself to the clerk and instructed him to ensure that the oath was taken a second time. The clerk repeated the question.

'I do,' said the defendant and then in the weakest of whispers to himself, 'I do in my hole.'

Evidence was heard and the defendant was asked if he had anything to say for himself. He denied extending his boundaries.

'I read in a book once,' he said to the judge, 'that bog does grow.'

'Yes,' said the judge, 'upwards at the rate of an inch or so every ten years but never outwards at the rate of an acre a year like yours.'

He was fined twenty pounds and ordered to draw back his paling sticks. I'll close now but in the next letter I'll tell you about that raid in Mayo. It happened shortly after De Valera's visit to Keeldown during a general election. Those were noisy and troublesome times.

> Love to all,
> Your fond uncle,
> Leo.

> G.S. Barracks,
> Monasterbawn.

Dear Joe:

I am enclosing a letter which I yesterday received from a woman who signs herself Hungry Home. From the contents you will see that she blames Fie's public house for the drinking habits of her husband. If he wants to drink he'll drink anyway and my raiding Fie's won't stop him.

He'll get it in any one of ten villages by merely mounting his cycle or thumbing a lift. I will now explain, to your satisfaction, about the alleged witchcraft in Monasterbawn graveyard. I know you're my superintendent but you should know better than to seek an explanation for such a disgraceful and unfounded accusation. It was the last night in November which, as you know, is the month of the Holy Souls. Around ten o'clock I went to the Widow Hansel's for a few pints and a game of thirty-one. The Widow shouted time at about quarter to twelve so we finished our drinks and made for the door. At the door Nance Hansel called me back.

'Leo,' she said, 'would you believe it's the last night of the Holy Souls and I haven't visited Oliver's grave yet.' Oliver Hansel, as you well know, was her husband.

'Is there any chance,' said she, 'that you'd accompany me till I say a prayer or two over the grave?'

I told her to be sure I would so off we set. It was twelve o'clock when we arrived at the graveyard gate. It was half past twelve and we leaving, it being a fine moonlight night and the Widow having several other relations to pray for, including her mother and father, aunts, uncles and whatnot. While she was praying I used to swing my arms back and forth and jump up and down to keep warm. That is the authentic account of the witchcraft and black magic which took place in Monasterbawn graveyard on the night of November the thirtieth in the year of our Lord nineteen hundred and seventy-five and may the good God perish the craven wretch who penned that infamous letter. I'll raid Fie's on Sunday night next and to keep the score even I will pay a call to Crutt's as well. I won't take names and I won't charge the publicans.

I don't like raiding public houses even when after-hours drinking goes on. Hard-working men and women deserve a drink or two at night if they so desire, provided they can afford it and provided that they do not blackguard their wives and families and leave them short. You're the super.

You know as well as I that there are no young people drinking here in Monasterbawn. They go to the towns and the city where they have no problem getting all the gin and vodka they want whether their ages are fourteen or eighteen. The drinkers in Monasterbawn are settled oldsters with those beastly exceptions who drink the weekly dole money and the family allowance and forget about home. The wives would be better off widows. They'd have the widow's pension and no one to take it from them.

When I first came here I foolishly believed that there were all sorts of orgies going on in public houses. I fell for the letters and the phone calls which are the bane of all guards' barracks in this green land. I set about cleaning things up. What a terrible mess I made in my ignorance. Sunday night was and is the best night for public house trade. There's life in the village from an early hour and there is the pleasant sound of music and singing and the deep hum of conversations coming from the doorways of the warm, companionable public houses. It was the one night which made life tolerable when I first came to Monasterbawn.

There was a bustle to the place. Men, woman and children walked the streets and would stand listening outside Crutt's before crossing to Fie's or going further down to Oliver Hansel's. There would be an occasional fight amongst the young bucks. No transport in those days so they were confined for their pleasures to the village. You might get a carload of townies out on a booze or have a window broken or have bicycles stolen but by and large it was a quiet enough place, all things allowed.

Sunday nights then and holy day nights were the only nights that the village permitted itself the luxury of rejoicing. Limited after-hours trading in the three pubs was taken for granted. In the spring, summer and autumn farmers and agricultural workers who lived in the vicinity were unable to come to town before nine or ten o'clock, particularly if the weather was fine. Neither would the villagers frequent the pubs until around the same hour. The man I replaced was an easy-going, popular Meathman who allowed this very lax situation to exist. He never went near the pubs and generally minded his own business unless specifically invited or incited to do otherwise. No doubt the man knew what he was doing. No one spoke ill of him after he left.

I should have followed his example. Instead I started to listen to stories and to believe the contents of the anonymous letters which came regularly, riddled with complaints about after-hours drinking and filled with character assassination and exaggerated accounts of normal, human behaviour. I raided Fie's first. I must say they were astonished. Mrs Fie went so far as to ask me why, as if she didn't know that after-hours drinking was illegal. Most of the customers escaped but I took the names of the others. These consisted mainly of old people or others who were too drunk or too lazy to run.

The following Sunday night I raided Crutt's and the Sunday night after I raided Oliver Hansel's, a premises which had not been raided in two generations. There was no one to shout stop. I was in the right and I knew for certain that many people approved.

The raids had no effect whatsoever on the after-hours trade. Neither had the fines imposed by the judge on the three publicans and their customers. A month later I struck again. I raided and cleared all three pubs on the same Sunday night. Convictions in the court followed. The customers hung around the street disconsolately for hours afterwards. Still they showed no resentment towards me.

The following Sunday night all three premises were at it hammer and tongs as if nothing had happened. I raided again and again and eventually there was no more after-hours trading on Sunday nights. Just to make sure I carried out one final raid. The pubs were closed, however, and my knocking was ignored. They were empty. I could testify to that.

The following Sunday night the village was deserted. Except for a few locals the pubs were deserted, their clientele scattered amongst the many other licensed premises at crossroads and villages not too far distant. A week later I was told that Jack Fie had gone to England to find work and that Crutt's was up for sale. Well they couldn't blame me could they? I was merely doing my duty. I convinced myself that I would be drawing money under false pretences if I did otherwise. Also I was responding to appeals from law-abiding people who felt that the law of the land was being flouted. On top of that I felt a new sense of authority. I must confess I was somewhat frightened by my power. The sad thing was I didn't look forward to Sunday nights anymore. There was no apparent change in the attitude of the village people towards me but at the newsagent's and the post office there was a tight rein on the conversation when I appeared. Then one Sunday night I met Oliver Hansel walking two of his greyhounds along the roadway. The loss of the after-hours trade had no effect whatsoever on him. He was a wealthy man, not dependant on the pub alone. He had a sizeable farm and, by all acounts, lashings of money. He had no family. If anything the closure was an asset because it have given him more time to train his dogs.

I bade him a good-night. He returned my salute civilly enough or so I thought. I fell into step beside him and we walked out of the village together, not saying anything, just enjoying the mildness of the summer night. I remember every word of our conversation as though it were yesterday. I daresay it was because Oliver was a man of few words and contrived to make these few memorable.

'The village is very dead in itself tonight,' I said in an effort to get conversation going. There was no answer. The dogs were squealing at some scent or other at the time. It was possible that he hadn't heard me.

'The village is very dead tonight,' I repeated.

'I heard you the first time,' he said without feeling of any kind. I decided to say no more after that. Then sudden-

30

ly he stopped dead in his tracks.

'If the village is dead,' he said without a trace of emotion, 'you're the man who must take the blame. It was you who murdered it.'

A week later Oliver Hansel was dead. He succumbed to a heart attack just as he was going to bed. He died in his wife's arms. His words stayed with me. Another week passed. Then on a day off I mounted my cycle and proceeded to the village of Derrymullane, nine miles away, to see a friend, one Jim Brick, a civic guard of thirty years standing. We often met in the course of our duty. His would be the nearest barracks to mine. His sergeant was a bit of a recluse who hated his job. Jim did most of the work.

'You know,' Jim said when I entered the day-room, 'I was more or less expecting you.' I told him about the raids but he already knew everything. He wouldn't be much of a policeman if he didn't. I told him what Oliver Hansel had said to me.

'He was never a man to say things lightly, the same Oliver,' Jim Brick said.

'Granted,' I replied, 'but you'll have to concede that all I was doing was applying the letter of the law.'

Jim remained silent for awhile, drawing on his pipe. Then, after a long pause he examined it closely and looked me in the eye.

'My dear Leo,' said he, 'applying the letter of the law when you are not a legal expert is like handling a Mill's bomb when you are not a bomb disposal expert. Both can blow up in your face when you least expect it.' I was about to interrupt but he waved his pipe in front of my face and continued.

'When the law does damage to the people it is supposed to benefit then the law has to be re-examined. The people who originally drew up the licensing laws did a fairly good job. They would, of course, have no way of knowing about villages like Monasterbawn or the situation that exists there. The solution, therefore, is to stretch the law as far as it will go. It will not stretch all that far but it nearly always stretches far enough provided we do not expect too much from it. I hope you are paying attention to what I am saying because I am giving you the benefits of thirty years front line experience. I could have been a commissioner if I so desired but my wife always said I was too brainy.

'Remember my dear Leo that, in many ways, the law is like a woman's knickers, full of dynamite and elastic and best left to those who have the legal right and qualifications to handle it properly.'

'So what am I to do?' I asked.

'Do nothing,' he advised. 'All scars heal, all wounds close. You have shown quite clearly that you are in charge of proceedings. Bide your time and do nothing. The drift back to the pubs will start sooner than you think. They'll naturally feel their way for a while but in a few months things will be back to normal. My advice is to leave well alone and keep a close eye on developments.'

I left Jim Brick a relieved man. Things turned out as he predicted. On Sunday nights now the village hums with trade and everyone is happy. In case they get too happy I will do as you suggest and give them a reminder but I would hate to see Monasterbawn returning to that forlorn state which I once created by innocently overplaying my hand.

Best regards to the missus. I'll convey your regards to Nance.

Yours obediently,
Garda Leo J. Molair.

Toormane Hill,
Monasterbawn.

Guard Molair:
That you might get V. D. D. V.

Signed,
A T.T.

My dear Ned:

Sorry for the delay. I have before me the shortest letter
ever received in these barracks. My guess is that it was sent
by Miss Lola Glinn, a shining light in the local branch of the
Pioneers' Total Abstinence Association. It has her crisp,
bitchy style and in addition she passed the graveyard the
night the Widow Hansel and myself were visiting it. She is
the chief danger to the pubs. She is capable of writing to
members of the government and to ministers, not to
mention supers, commissioners and assistant commissioners.
The chief reason is her father, a harmless poor devil who
fancies a few pints on Saturday and Sunday nights. He is,
alas, unable to carry more than three pints. After that he
has to be helped home but he's not a nuisance and he
offends nobody. The villagers always keep an eye out for
him. For a while the pubs stopped serving him but they
became sorry when they saw the forlorn cut of him and he
staring through their windows.

About that raid in Mayo. It's a long time ago now. As I
recall it was a fine autumn night. The air was crisp with frost
and in the village of Keeldown where Mick Drea and myself
were stationed there was an air of tension and excitement.
De Valera was expected to speak on behalf of his party's
candidate and our sergeant, Matt Bergin, had us on our toes
hours before the event. We were to watch out for suspicious
characters who might be entertaining notions of assassination and to make sure that the village square was clear of
all obstructions. We had the help of three other guards and
an inspector who was just after getting promotion. Every
window he passed he squinted in to admire his reflection.
He was much like a gorsoon after being presented with a
new pair of shoes.

At eight o'clock the first of the crowd began to arrive.
Dev wasn't due until ten but there were many admirers of
his who wanted a good position near the platform where

they could be close to him. I never knew a man who could inspire so much genuine love and provoke so much vicious hatred at the same time. Our sergeant hated the sight of him. We would often be sitting happily in the day-room when unexpectedly Dev's name would be mentioned on the radio in connection with some statement of policy or visit abroad. Our sergeant would rise and spit out and then leave the room without a word. On the other hand if Dev's name was mentioned while Mick Drea was wearing his cap the cap would come off at once and Mick would hold it across his chest with a radiant look in his eyes. That was Dev, the devil incarnate in the eyes of Matt Bergin and a saint in the eyes of Mick Drea. I won't attempt to analyse him. All I will say is that his visit to Keeldown turned out to be the most colourful event that village ever knew before or since. At nine you couldn't draw a leg in the pubs and by half-past nine the square was thronged. There were several nasty fist fights. There would be a reference to Dev's ancestry and the man who made it would be asked to repeat what he said by some other hothead. Then the clipping started. It gave us all we could do to prevent a minor war. At ten a rumour swept through the crowd that he was in the outskirts but it was unfounded because almost an hour was to pass before he would make his appearance. Finally he arrived. He already had a bodyguard but we took up our positions at either side of his immediate entourage to keep back the crowd. In front of the procession were one hundred men in double file. These carried uplifted four-prong pikes on top of which were blazing sods of turf which had earlier been well steeped in paraffin. The bearers of these torches were grim-faced and military-like men and boys of all ages. Behind them were two score of horsemen and to parody these there were several asses, mules and small ponies mounted by youngsters and drunken farmer's boys. Next came the Keeldown fife and drum band playing *O'Donnell Abu*. Then came a brass band playing *The Legion of the Rearguard*. It was a circus of a kind that would have

34

delighted the heart of Barnum. Dev, the ringmaster, never batted an eyelid. After the brass band came a number of village idiots, local drunkards, bums, characters, clowns and an assortment of other irresponsible wretches to whom an occasion like this is meat and drink. After this contingent came the major attraction, the man himself flanked by local dignitaries, ministers and T.D.'s. He walked with his head erect, body rigid and with no trace of a smile on his pointed face. His dark felt hat and long black overcoat became him as they became no other man I ever saw. He looked as if he carried the whole weight of the country on his shoulders and who am I to say whether he did or not.

'Look at the strut of the whore,' Matt Bergin whispered, 'and the innocent blood still reeking from his hands.'

'Wash your mouth out,' Mick Drea whispered with suppressed fury. 'He is the saviour of our country, the greatest Irishman since Saint Patrick.'

'But Saint Patrick wasn't an Irishman,' I said innocently.

'Neither is Dev,' Matt whispered triumphantly. The procession continued. Behind the celebrities came the members of the local brigade of the old I.R.A. They must have numbered two hundred.

'Where in the name of God did they all come from?' Matt asked sarcastically.

'They're good men and true,' said Mick.

'Maybe so,' Matt retaliated, 'but where the hell were they when the Black and Tans were here?'

They marched solemn-faced and sombre without looking to left or right. Sometimes they were taunted and jeered. Other times they were cheered. They showed no reaction whatsoever. Here, for one night only, were men of action, of steely resolve, men to be reckoned with. Tomorrow the carnival would be over and for several years until Dev's next visit they would revert to their natural roles of small farmer, labourer, clerk, tradesman and unemployed. Tonight was theirs. They were expressing unity and solidarity in the presence of the chief whom they adored and revered as no man was revered since O'Connell or Jesus Christ himself. The old I.R.A. were followed by a throng of ordinary supporters and hundreds of others who came out of curiosity merely to have a glimpse at the Man of Destiny. Hundreds more from the opposition came to scoff and jeer or maybe to engage in a spot of heckling although they would want to ensure that they were out of clouting distance of the more rabid Fianna Fail supporters. As the procession entered the square a great cry arose from the multitude. The Irish people have always been caught short for leaders of quality and when they were presented with De Valera they clung to him for dear life.

He attracted the most extraordinary and contradictory collection of people that ever assembled to pay homage to the same person. There were tycoons, priests, nuns and professional men rubbing shoulders with illiterates, semi-illiterates, half-wits and stunted unfortunates, the personification of utter poverty. Allegiance to Dev or to Cosgrave was often the cause of violent rows and lifelong bitterness between neighbours. Matt Bergin insists that De Valera was alone responsible for the Civil War and its horrific bloodshed.

'He was the cause of it,' Matt insisted, 'because he could have stopped it and failed to do so.'

What Matt overlooked was that Dev certainly gave the poorer elements new life and hope and pride in themselves, a quality lacking in the vast majority of the Irish people for ages. In the square the air reeked of paraffin. The crowd were chanting now as Dev climbed on to the platform. An aged, shawled woman clung to him, kissing his hand. He good-naturedly pushed her to one side. Others wept when they touched his hands or clothes. At the base of the platform were the most vocal of all, a band of craven bums whose loyalty could be bought for a bottle of stout. These were pushed away by stewards to make way for the real supporters. When Dev came forward to speak men and women in the crowd wept openly. Others held infant children aloft that they might get a glimpse of the great

man and have it to say to their children that once they saw
the Man of Destiny. There was frenzy now in the square as
he laid allegation after allegation against the opposition.
Emotions were at fever pitch. On the edge of the crowd a
fierce fight broke out and we had to draw our batons to
prevent its spreading. There were hundreds of wild-eyed,
crazed patriots spoiling for mayhem. Fortunately, it ended
peacefully. Afterwards the pubs were jammed and throngs
of troublemakers infested the lanes and streets. We had a
busy time maintaining law and order. At about one o'clock
in the morning, long after Dev had departed, the inspector
informed us that we were to clear the pubs.

'I want the job done thoroughly,' he said, 'and I want
the job done now or there will be repercussions.'

So saying he got into his car and left the dirty work to
us. One by one we cleared them of customers until only
one remained. This was the property of a local county
councillor. I knew it would not be easy to clear the place
but justice would have to be seen to be done or the guards
would be the talk of the place the following day.

'You do the back,' I told Mick, 'and I'll do the front.'
The sergeant had gone to bed at this stage. We had no
intention of prosecuting. Our only aim was to clear the
place as peacefully as possible, it being the night it was. I
made my way into the thick of the thronged bar and then
as loud as I could I made my intentions clear. I could also
hear Mick's voice coming from the kitchen. Suddenly the
proprietor was fuming by my side.

'What the hell do you think you're doing?' he shouted.

'My duty,' I replied.

'What's the trouble?' The question came from a burly,
well-dressed man who I recognised as a T.D. of considerable
prominence and a man who was tipped for a ministry
should Dev win the election.

'This fellow wants to clear the house,' the proprietor
informed him.

'Eff off out of here fast you Free State shagger,' said the

politician, 'or I'll have you transferred to Timbuctoo.'

'I am a Guard on public house duty,' I said as calmly as I could, 'acting on the instructions of my inspector. I am now ordering you to leave these premises.'

'And if I don't go,' he said with menace. There was a deadly silence at this stage with all present clinging to every word. This was a show-down. There could be no back-down. I found Mick Drea standing beside me.

'If you don't leave peacefully I will remove you forcibly,' I told him.

'You blueshirt bastard,' he shouted and he swung a fist at me. I ducked and spun him around and then propelled him out of the pub. Meanwhile Mick had drawn his baton in case some of his supporters decided to take part. Rather than risk prosecution the publican decided to co-operate. The repercussions came at once. The following morning I was visited by the Chief Superintendent who asked me for a full account of what happened. The politician had rung him up first thing that morning demanding my dismissal from the force. The super heard me out.

'Write him a letter of apology,' he suggested. 'It's sure to mollify him.'

'Apology for what?' I asked.

'Please don't be difficult,' said the super.

'I can't apologise for something I didn't do,' I told him. He rose to go.

'Write that letter today,' he said.

Immediately I rang my own district super and told him the score.

'There's little I can do Leo,' he said, 'except to promise you that I will oppose any move to transfer you.'

Transferred I was, not to Timbuctoo but here to Monasterbawn, less than thirty miles from the place where I was born. Instead of punishing me the politician, in his ignorance, had done me a favour.

Love to Gert and little Eddie. Write soon.

> Your fond uncle,
> Leo.

Dear Leo:

After you left the last day himself made one of his rare appearances in the day-room and asked who the visitor was. I told him it was yourself.

'I am your sergeant,' he said. 'All these matters must be reported.'

He then ordered a full turn-out for inspection of every garda in the barracks. I turned out smartly and this seemed to satisfy him. He went back upstairs talking to himself. He has me in a terrible state but he's harmless for the most part. He doesn't do a stroke of work, just goes out to eat and comes back when it suits him. Luckily the work is light and I can manage on my own but one of these days I will have to make a discreet report to Superintendant Fahy (Call-me-Joe). There is always the danger that things might get out of hand and who knows but the locals might start pinking off letters to higher places. I'll keep an eye on him as best I can. If I send for you come running as we don't want a scandal.

Yesterday he was particularly grouchy and warned me that he would not stand for insubordination. Upstairs with him then and on goes the talk. This time there was loud laughter as well and I became worried so I crept upstairs. There were other voices. I could hear them quite plainly. However, when I peeped in the keyhole I could see nobody but himself. He was addressing himself to two imaginary gentlemen who occupied two chairs facing the table where he sat. He would speak for a while and then listen to what the others had to say. When he had digested their remarks he would throw back the head and laugh to his heart's content. It was all quite harmless but the danger was that Mrs Hussey the char might make an appearance requesting instructions. She lives down the street and comes for an hour or two every day.

He poured out imaginary drinks for his two friends and then listened to some news of great import. He nodded his head from time to time and his face grew more serious as the talk went on. When the address was finished he banged the table with his fist and shouted hurrah several times. Then he started to weep but not for long. Manfully he wiped his eyes and rose from his seat. He saluted smartly and shook hands with his two visitors. I crept downstairs again and he started to show them to the door. He led them down and in the hallway there was some more banter and loud laughter. Out on to the street with him then where he shook hands with the pair, embracing both in turn as he did so. He then carefully banged the door of the car and waved goodbye. He was so convincing that I could almost hear the engine running. Luckily it was raining cats and dogs at the time and there was nobody on the street. He came into the day-room rubbing his hands. He put his back to the fire and eyed me in a friendly way for the first time in years.

'Why didn't you come up Jim?' he said.

'Up where?' said I.

'Upstairs to meet the lads,' said he.

'What lads?' said I.

'The assistant commissioner and the minister,' said he.

'I know my place,' said I.

'Ah well now,' he said magnanimously, 'the lads wouldn't have have minded. They're just like ourselves man.'

'Why didn't the commissioner come?' I asked.

'Jealousy Mick. Jealousy boy.'

I shook my head sympathetically.

'There's nothing he can do now except scratch himself. My promotion has been sanctioned by the minister.'

'Does this mean I'll be calling you inspector from now on?' I asked.

'You'll be calling me superintendent,' he said proudly. 'Apparently they have heard of my work at headquarters and want me up there with them.'

'When will you be leaving?' I asked.

'That's entirely up to myself. I'll have to straighten out a few things here first before I decide upon a time.'

He remained silent for a long while after this announcement so I returned to my work. The next thing he threw a fiver on the table. 'Get a drink for the lads,' he said, 'and tell them there's no hurry back. I'll hold the fort here.'

He went upstairs and after a short while I heard him pacing to and fro. I took the fiver and had three large whiskies in case I'd go out of my mind. Say nothing about all this to anyone. Just say a prayer that I can handle the situation when the inevitable happens.

As always,
Jim Brick.

P. S. You may be wondering if he was always like this. I suppose you could say he was always a little odd. However, for the past year he has been showing signs of going off the head altogether. I don't know what triggered it off. I believe he was let down by a good-looking girl one time in his youth. That wouldn't be any help to him. What may have got him going was a visit we had from a lady here about a year ago. Her son had broken into the local presbytery and struck the Canon with a timber crucifix he took from the wall. A touch of religious mania. Anyway the Canon who played football for the county in his youth gave the fellow a shot in the gut and put him on the flat of his back. We locked him up, gave him his supper and retired to the dayroom where we had work in plenty. It was a quiet winter's night as I recall. The wind howled outside but we had a good fire. Suddenly the door burst open and our prisoner's mother stood there with a crazed look in her eye.

'Where's my boy?' she screeched. 'Which one of you two rotten bastards has taken my baby?'

The baby, of course, was twenty-two years of age but it was hardly the time to point this out to her. She was obviously in a demented state and I detected a strong smell of whiskey.

'Give me back my boy,' she screamed at the top of her voice. 'Take me but give me back my son.' With that she

41

ups with the front of her skirt. My eyes nearly popped out of my head. Not a screed of a knickers or bloomers of any kind did she wear. The sergeant was transfixed to his chair like a man who had been struck dumb. She lifted the skirt higher and stood directly in front of the sergeant revealing as fine a brush of jet-black hair as ever sprung from the base of a female belly. He sat transfixed, his mouth opened, utterly shocked out of his wits.

'Release my child,' she cried out in drunken frenzy, 'and do with my body what you will.'

'Missus,' said I, 'go home and have the grace of God about you and we'll put in a good word for your son when the hearing comes up.'

She dropped her skirt. 'Scum,' she screamed. 'Scum in uniform.' In the end I succeeded in getting her out. I locked the door behind her. She screamed and shrieked for a short while and then went off when nobody came to listen to her. When I returned to the day-room my man was still in a state of shock from the spectacle he had seen. He must never have seen the likes before, being a bit of a celibate and all that.

I'll have to sign off Leo. I hear him coming downstairs, no doubt for inspection.

As always,
Jim.

* * *

The life of an unmarried civic guard, solitary custodian of the peace in a remote village, can be lonely in the extreme yet Leo Molair was not a lonely man. Neither is he a bored man. Regarding the people in his bailiwick he could be a mine of information but he choses to keep all that is not relevant to law and order closely to himself and is as careful about revealing information concerning his charges as a priest or doctor. He listens and says nothing even when he disbelieves the outrageous concoctions which the villagers invent about each other. His power lies in his willingness to listen and later to reject or absorb what he has heard. He is perhaps the most respected figure in the area. Of enemies he has his share. He would be a poor policeman if he hadn't. Of friends he has many and of close friends his fair quota. Not since his Dublin days has Leo been intimate with a woman. His relationship with Nance Hansel is a purely platonic one. As far as he is concerned it would never amount to anything more than a cosy chat or a day out with the other regulars. His plans for the future are carefully laid. He owns a site on the mountain road. Here he plans to build a small chalet on his retirement. He is happy in his work and can have no way of knowing that the real crises of his life loom ahead of him. We find him now writing to his superintendent.

*   *   *

Monasterbawn,
Co. Cork.

Dear Joe:

As usual the crowds arrived into the village on Sunday night last and as usual the pubs started to fill up around ten o'clock which is closing time as you well know. I raided Fie's first and cleared the house of forty-seven customers. Mrs Fie asked me the very same question she asked me when I first raided her nearly twenty years ago.

'Why?'

'Because missus,' said I, 'it's against the law.'

''Tis a cracked law,' said she, 'that closes the pubs at the very hour the people wants a drink.'

'I didn't make the law missus,' I reminded her.

'I hope,' said she, 'that you will clear out that brothel across the road.' I assured her that nobody would be neglec-

43

ted. I also told her that while I continued receiving letters I would continue to raid the pubs. Unable to conceal her astonishment she asked for clarification.

'You must understand Mrs Fie,' said I, 'that when I get a letter complaining of one pub it means that all have to be raided. For instance if tomorrow I receive a letter complaining about after-hours trade in Crutt's it does not mean that the other pubs are immune. Far from it. My super would expect me to make a clean sweep of all three licensed premises in Monasterbawn so that everybody might see that the law has no favourites.'

This set her thinking. We can only wait and see if it will have the desired effect. Next I raided Crutt's who hadn't the good sense to clear the house while I was engaged with Fie's. There were seventy-one customers on the premises. All made their escape without difficulty. I explained to Mrs Crutt about the letters. She agreed it was a disgraceful thing entirely for one publican to write in to the barracks complaining about another.

'And they call themselves Christians,' she said with a look of outrage on her face. I left her and proceeded towards the Widow's but that cute creature had taken the hint and cleared the house while Crutt's was being raided. She would have had a few customers, possibly a dozen or so old topers of my own age. It was the company rather than the business that induced her to keep the place open at all. I drank a hasty half one and a pint before making a final tour of the village for the night.

In Jackass Lane I encountered several courting couples but there is no law against this so I passed them by bidding each pair a goodnight. From Tremble's shack came the sound of discord. Drawing nearer I could hear Mocky's voice raised in anger and the screams of his wife from time to time. I pushed the door open and there was Mocky and he having the poor woman by the throat. The children were huddled in a corner. What a start to life. I broke Mocky's grip on his long-suffering partner and dragged him outside. I

44

slapped his face for a while. There was no other way to sober him up and there was no point in charging him with assault because the wife wouldn't testify against him. I lugged him back to the barracks and locked him in the cell for a while. Later when he would be sober I might allow him home. I continued on my tour of inspection. At the foot of the Mountain Road I saw a figure in front of me. It was none other than Goggles Finn, the local Peeping Tom and the biggest general nuisance in the whole district. This time he was peeping in the window of a house owned by a middle-aged lady whose name was Aggie Boucher. This surprised me somewhat for Aggie has a figure like a sack of spuds and a face to match. When I tiptoed up behind Goggles Finn, Aggie was disrobing for bed. There was a light on in the room and nothing was left to the imagination. She stripped to the skin and took her time about it. I tapped Goggles on the shoulder. He let a scream out of him that could be heard at the other end of the village. Without looking around he ran for his life up the Mountain Road, screeching like a scalded cat.

Aggie Boucher, in a nightdress and coat with her hair in curlers, appeared all of a sudden in her doorway.

'What's going on out there?' she called angrily.

'Goggles Finn,' I explained.

'What about him?' she asked.

'He was peeping at you,' I called back.

'Don't you think I know that you goddam interfering get,' she said. I went away chastened.

I'll close for now.

As ever,
Leo.

Fallon Street G.S.,
Dublin 13.

Dear Uncle Leo:
Superintendent Conners arrived this morning and instruct-

45

ed me to forget about some summonses I was preparing for a gentleman who parked his car on three different occasions outside a hospital entrance. I was about to object and to point out the incalculable amount of trouble this man had caused not to mention all the cost to the state and all the time involved when he cut me short.

'There are exceptional circumstances involved here,' he said. 'Just do as I say like a good man.'

Ours is not to reason why. Mick Drea says the car owner must be well-up in the world, probably a member of the same golf club as Patcheen but my sergeant says it is quite possible that the man may have been of considerable service to the guards on occasion and on this account we cannot be too critical. What do you think? Also tell me about Big Morto McNeal who Mick Drea says once drank a firkin of porter in the round of a day. Often too the old boys here talk about a guard called Flash Muldook and about his fatal charm for women.

Gert and young Eddie are grand altogether.

That's all for now,

Your found nephew,
Ned.

Garda Station,
Monasterbawn.

Dear Ned:

First of all let us look at Patcheen and the summonses. You would be best advised not to question your super's actions no matter how provocative or irresponsible they may seem to be. What the hell bloody use is there in being a super if you can't do a turn for a friend. So long as he doesn't over-do it you have no option but to play along. Take your brothers-in-law now. Wouldn't you be the hard-hearted man if you turned one of them down after he asking you to square the parking summons. Try and put yourself in

46

Patcheen's place. A super has to use discretion and he needs to have the more influential of the public favourably disposed towards the law. Ninety-five per cent of the time our supers go by the book and that's more than can be said for any police force anywhere.

My own super here now is a great character so long as you remember who is boss. Like the Bishop of Kerry he likes to be called by his first name which in his case is Joe. The wife is also a great character. My man is not a squarer of summonses but he will be moved by the plea of a decent man or woman or honest, hard-working parents. When the strict enforcement of the rules is likely to do more harm than good he will know the right move to make. No better man to have a few jars with and no better man to back up those under his command but tell him the truth and don't come the smart Alec with him or he'll nail you to the cross. As long as he knows what's going on all is well but when he doesn't know life can be a misery for the whole district. For instance if he hears something second-hand he'll eff and blind all-comers indiscriminately until he cools down. However, when you meet a new-made super who's just a natural-born bastard dig in your heels and work to rule. The novelty of his new found authority will wear off after a specified time. Remember that so long as we of the rank and file stick together we are the real bosses no matter what anybody says.

You ask about big Murto McNeal. Of all the uncommon, unlikely, uncivilised, uncouth, unmannerly sons of bitches this was the pure-bred, pedigreed champion. Of course he'd never get into the guards now. He was rammed in after the Economic War by a T.D. who should have known better. Some say he was the bastard brother of a minister of state. Murdo was six feet five inches tall, weighed nineteen stone with a big fat red face not unlike a prize boar. He was never seen to spend a single shilling in his entire life. He handed every last penny of his wages over to his wife Minnie. Minnie the Pom she was nicknamed. She was puny, poisonous and bitter. You wouldn't notice her alongside Murto. Neighbours used to say that she slept on top of him lest he suffocate her by accident some night. My first meeting with Big Murto McNeal was at a guards' dance in Mayo. He never paid for the tickets. He just told a publican who was doing a prosperous after-hours trade that he would like two tickets for himself and the Pom. I happened to be sitting at the same table as the pair of them. There were sixteen people to each table. Murto consumed three separate dinners and then he noticed a large plate of buns in the centre of the table. These had been placed there earlier to go with the tea which would be served after the meal. Murto reached across a huge hand and grabbed the plate.

'Christ boys what have ye agin' these?' he asked with a huge smile. With that he placed the plate on his lap and he swallowed every last one of those buns as if they were crumbs. It's true he drank a firkin of porter once. It was at the wake of a well-known publican. The wake lasted all night and since it was a talkative town the guards could not very well be seen to be taking intoxicating drinks while on duty. The publican's son very considerately called Murto aside and told him that he would he placing a tapped firkin of porter especially for the guards in a comfortable outhouse at the rear of the premises.

'The Lord have mercy on the dead,' said Murto. 'There is no guard in this district but won't be praying for your father.'

The barrel was duly taken out by the son and left on a handy perch inside the door with glasses galore and a bottle of good quality whiskey for starters. The first thing Murto did was to go to the outhouse and consume half the whiskey direct from the bottle. Periodically afterwards he would visit the outhouse and lower a few pints preceded, of course, by a snort of the hot stuff. Murto saw to it that no other guard was informed about either the whiskey or the porter. He came off duty at six in the morning. He went immediately to the outhouse where he took off his cap and coat in order to get down to the business of serious drinking. At eleven o'clock in the day he was discovered fast asleep by a mourner who had inadvertently mistaken the outhouse for the lavatory. Murto slept with his mouth wide open and the deep snores came rumbling upwards like thunder from the caverns of his throat. The publican's son was alerted but the joint attempts of both men were not sufficient to wake him. Finally a horse and rail was sent for. It took the combined efforts of seven men to load him into the rail. When this was done his body was covered with tarpaulin and he was taken home. The owner of the horse and rail went to the rear of Murto's house, heeled his car and unloaded his cargo, without ceremony, outside the backdoor. He then kicked the door hard and long and took off as fast as he could in case the Pom might think he had been Murto's drinking companion. How she got him into the house was a mystery. Some say she used an old window shutter as a lever and bit by bit managed to ease him inside. There she covered him with a quilt and a blanket and left him until he was obliged to go on duty that night. He woke hours later with a flaming head but reported for duty nevertheless. He touched several of his colleagues for money but got none. No one had money in those days except a few shopkeepers and professional people such as doctors and lawyers and the like. Anyway he never paid back what he borrowed. He bided his time until midnight. Then he started to raid the pubs. From every one he exacted his toll. He would first knock gently at the public house door. He knew the secret knock of every one. When the publican would open up and peer out expecting to see a familiar face Murto would whisper: 'Guards on public house duty.'

'Would you drink a pint?' the publican would ask.

'Would I drink a pair of 'em,' from Murto. He employed this tack on all the pubs which were engaged in after-hours trade until his head was cured and his belly full of free porter. If any publican refused him a drink he summonsed him on the spot. He had the longest reach I ever saw in a human being if there was anything to be grabbed that cost nothing. When he was in digs he had a boarding-house reach to outclass all boarding-house reaches. If another diner took his eyes off his plate for a split second Murto's huge paw would descend on the plate and sweep whatever was on it. When the astonished victim looked around to see who had taken his supper Murto's face would be the picture of innocence. He had no time for colleagues who were under six feet in height.

'Small guards is no good for nothing except small women,' he would say. It was said of him that he drank thirty pints of porter give or take a few pints every day for thirty years which was no mean achievement when you consider that he did not pay for a single pint. He would call for a drink alright when in company but somebody else always paid for it. It's a sad fact about many unfortunate people in this country but they will insist upon buying drink for guards even if it means going without food for themselves and their families. Murto and his equals always took advantage of these people. On the other hand it was and is an acute source of embarrassment to most guards who like to buy their own drink and be beholden to nobody. Poor Murto. He could never get enough of strong drink. He passed from this hard world at the tender age of sixty-one, only one year before he was due to retire. He was on temporary duty at a village carnival where he was not known to the proprietors of the public houses. At midnight, acting on orders from the local sergeant, Murto and a few other guards started to clear the pubs. The sergeant meant business so there was no way Murto could come around free drink. The last pub they raided was owned by a widow who had never seen Murto before in her life. Murto was well aware of this and as he was leaving the premises he took hold of his forehead and staggered all over the place moaning painfully.

'Oh my poor man,' said the widow, 'what ails you?' Murto made no answer but he pointed dramatically at his chest. The widow at once went inside the counter where she seized a bottle of brandy and a glass. She poured a full tumbler and held it to Murto's mouth. He was now seated on a chair with his hand inside the tunic. He swallowed in dribs and drabs until he had the measure inside of him. The widow in her innocence filled the glass again. This time Murto took the glass in his own hands.

'Do whatever you have to do,' he told the widow. 'I'll sit here awhile till the pain goes.'

The widow, it transpired, had to go to the outskirts of the village to collect her two daughters who were attending a dance in the marquee which had been specially erected for the duration of the carnival.

'Go away cratur,' said Murto magnanimously. 'I'll hould the fort till you get back.'

'Help yourself to what drink you want,' said the widow. 'I won't be long.'

'I might try another small sup so,' he called out weakly. When he was alone he polished off the contents of the brandy bottle and liking the taste of it went inside the counter where he found a second bottle. What happened in the meanwhile was that the widow, as soon as she stuck her head inside the entrance to the marquee, was asked to dance. Knowing the house was in safe hands she waited till the ball was over. When she returned there was no sign of Murto or of two full bottles of brandy which was the widow's entire stock of that wonderful amber liquid.

It was Seán O'Conlon of the Special Branch who pieced together what happened afterwards. It would seem that Murto consumed the brandy in question in less than forty-five minutes. On his way back to the barracks he found himself weakening so he entered a meadow where he sat for a spell with his back to a cock of hay. After a while he fell asleep full stretch on his stomach. Around three o'clock in the morning he swallowed his tongue and was suffocated. God be good to him. He wasn't the worst of them. We shall not look upon his likes again, not in the uniform of a civic

51

guard at any rate. Remind me sometime to tell you about the two women who proposed to myself and Mick Drea.

My love to Gert and the child.

Your fond uncle,
Leo.

Super's Office,
District Headquarters, G. S.

Dear Leo:

Good man yourself. I am most happy with your report. Monasterbawn has never given me any headaches thanks to you. From the point of view of peace and quiet it could be looked upon as the showpiece of the district. I note from your latest dispatch that you intend coming out next year. I am fully aware of the fact that you are entitled to retire anytime you like but I would ask you, as a personal favour, to reconsider. This district needs men of your calibre. Think about it. I spent the first ten years of my career in a village no bigger than Monasterbawn. I had a sergeant who was always at his wit's end trying to restrain me. I knew it all, of course, in those days. But for that sergeant I wouldn't have lasted three months in the force. He was a father and mother to me. At first I couldn't understand why he ignored most of my reports or why he would pooh-pooh what I regarded as vital information. As time passed I began to appreciate his wisdom. The first boob I made was to arrest a man I found climbing over the back wall of a garden which surrounded a handsome detached house on the outskirts of the village. I lugged him straight to the barracks despite all his protestations. I demanded a statement from him but he demanded to see the sergeant. What an awkward, uncooperative scoundrel he was. The sergeant appeared in his pyjamas.

'Go home Jim,' he told my prisoner.

'Thanks Pat,' said he and out of the door with him. I ranted and fumed after that and for weeks there was a coolness between us. How dare he dismiss my valiant efforts with a few words, without even consulting me. A month later I caught the same man climbing over the same garden wall. I arrested him a second time and took him to the barracks. Again the sergeant appeared and again he told my captive to go home. After that we didn't speak for three months except in the line of business. What a fool I was. Every week without fail I would see the same man climbing over the same wall. It took me years to discover that he was a local farmer, the hen-pecked husband of a sexless and careless wife. He was a decent sort of man despite his aberrations. The woman he was visiting was a boxom, sexy-looking lady in her forties who lived with her married sister and whose small back room overlooked the wall which her lover so often climbed. Everybody knew what was going on except the man's wife and myself. After that I wasn't half as brash or officious. I learned that nightfall, as far as a civic guard was concerned, was but the overture to another sorry opus on the human situation, another chapter in the mighty tome of human lunacy. I often despaired of the human race after a month of nights. Even in that tiny village the hours of darkness were filled with shuffling, silent shapes which were identifiable after a while as prominent or common or worthless members of the community. Night-time is for lovers, lawbreakers and cats. Sometimes on misty, chilly winter nights I would pass a pair of lovers intent on their kissing and cuddling in a shady place off the beaten track. I'm ashamed to say curiosity often got the better of me and I would draw aside as soon as they parted from each other in order to see who they were. I was once shocked to the core for the woman was the respectable mother of a family. I ceased to be shocked thereafter and I would take it in my stride, the rare time I would see a married woman of impeccable character, dressed in raincoat and headscarf, furtively scurrying homewards from the arms of another man. I learned too that there were reasons for this kind of carry-on. not good reasons but reasons all the same, often almost

53

amounting to justification. It might be spite for an uncaring spouse or revenge on an unfaithful partner or it could be that some foolish woman had fallen for the looks and lingo of a Casanova. Often it would be love, pure and unadorned. I was the only witness to the isolated and uncommon. Happily for those whose paths crossed mine in the dark of the night I was a witness who would never testify. A layman with whom I was once drinking insisted, during the course of our conversation, that civic guards were dour, uncommunicative fellows who seemed reluctant to join in normal conversation. An exaggeration, of course, but not without a grain of truth. I tried to explain to him that a man who knows so much about the people of his community has to be cautious when communicating with others lest he slip up and bring somebody into disrepute. This he refused to accept saying that guards should let their hair down the same as everybody else. Personally speaking my experience is that it pays to be careful and conservative when conversing with members of the general public. Personal opinions Leo are a luxury which you and I just cannot afford.

I'll wind up now but not before I compliment you on the fine job you're doing in Monasterbawn. I wish you would not look upon the difference in our ranks as an excuse for not calling to see me when you're in town. There's always a bed here for you. Give my regards to the Widow Hansel and keep up the splendid work.

As ever,
Joe Fahy.

Toormane Hill,
Monasterbawn.

Guard Molair:
Raid the Widow's and do us all a favour by catching yourself. Do something about the young drunkards who shout and yell on their way home at night. Scum is what you are

and a low tinker to boot. Be careful don't you give the Widow a child, and try to have the grace of God about you.

Signed,
A T.T.

Garda Barracks,
Monasterbawn.

Dear Ned:

Many thanks for yours of yesterday. I see by the papers that O'Connell Street is dominated at night by young thugs. Too much is expected of the guards. How can a handful subdue a horde when the public looks on and for the most part enjoys it. You can't have law and order without consent from the public. Without their back-up the uniform is only a target for thugs. God forbid me but I loathe gangs whether they be religious, political or sporting. You'll find when you sort them out that there isn't a good man in the bunch. Your decent man won't run with gangs no matter what their purpose. Good men don't form gangs. Only the scum of the earth do that.

You ask about Flash Maldook. Well what they say is true. He was the greatest ladies man since Casanova and having a guard's uniform was no disadvantage to him. The women loved him, married, single or otherwise. He had a pencil moustache, dark brown eyes and curly black hair on top of a head that was without a brain of any kind. He was a handsome scoundrel however. Make no mistake about that. When he flashed those white teeth of his and shook his head so that his curls danced on the rim of his forehead few women could resist him. It was a woman who got him into the guards. In those days you didn't need much education. She was the Reverend Mother of the local convent in the town where Flash resided. The poor woman went on her knees to the local sergeant to get him out of town. Damage had been already done to two of her pupils and the party responsible was our friend Flash Maldook. The sergeant groomed him for the guards and eventually he got him in. As I said already the uniform crowned him. Even if he had wanted to he couldn't keep the females away. As fond as the women were of Flash he was even fonder of them. He lasted a year. He was forced to flee to Canada after it was discovered that a score of pregnant women had named him as the sole cause of their predicaments. He was a legend in his own time. They say that women swooned when he entered a dance-hall and the whispers would spread like wildfire; 'Maldook is here. Maldook is here.' Some say he was shot dead by a jealous husband in Montreal while more say he joined an order of monks and devoted his life to God as an atonement for his sins. You won't knock an old dog off his track and what I say is that Flash Maldook is still fornicating with females whether in Alaska or Nebraska, whether white, black, mottled or brown.

One thing is sure. He sired them on the tops of mountains and the depths of valleys, up against hall doors and halfdoors, against hawthorn hedges, turf-ricks and oatstacks, in rain or shine, on dry ground and puddle, in the backs of motorcars and in the fronts of motorcars, upstairs and downstairs, in haysheds and turfsheds, byres and barns, in nooks and crannies and all over the place till he transported himself through necessity across the wide Atlantic. I'll close now. I see my friend Jerry Fogg, the postman, at the window. I wonder what brings him at this late hour. There's trouble. It's written clearly on his face. It's bad trouble. Jerry wouldn't look like that unless there was death in the background. I'll conclude.

Your fond uncle,
Leo.

P. S. I was right. All hell has broken loose here. A husband and wife on their way home to their abode a mile from Monasterbawn were knocked down and killed by a car which did not stop. A few moments ago Mocky Trembles of Jackass Lane stumbled across the bodies. I'll close. Say a prayer for us.

Uncle Leo.

Garda Barracks,
Monasterbawn.

Dear Superintendent Fahy:

Here is the report as requested. At twelve minutes past twelve on the morning of 11 April it was brought to my attention by local postman Jerry Fogg that a serious accident had taken place in the roadway known as Jackass Lane which is the only northern approach to the village of Monasterbawn. I proceeded immediately to the spot and there beheld two bodies, both lying approximately on the middle of the roadway and exactly thirty-one feet apart. They were the bodies of a man and a woman known to me as John and Sheila Glenn, husband and wife and the parents of six young children whose ages range from four months to ten years. Upon examination I perceived that they were both dead or as like to dead as I could make out. Priest and doctor had already been sent for. There were forty-feet brake marks at the right side of the roadway and a foot long torchlight which had apparently been in use by the deceased was still switched on when I discovered it on the grass margin near where Mrs Glenn lay. I instructed the postman Fogg to notify the district headquarters by the barracks phone while I remained on the scene of the accident to take comprehensive measurements by tape.

At twelve twenty-nine Doctor Bawney, the local M.O. and coroner, arrived on the scene. After a brief inspection he ordered the bodies to be removed to his surgery where, after a thorough examination he pronounced John and Sheila Glenn dead. A ambulance removed the bodies to the mortuary of Ballincarra district hospital, it being the nearest such place to the scene of the accident. Attached find two copies of the coroner's report.

Signed,
Officer in charge
Monasterbawn, G. S.,
Leo Molair.

Personal.

Dear Joe:

For the love and honour of God will you do all in your power to prevent what looks all set to be a massive inflow of garda personnel. I know this area like the back of my hand and I can tell you straight that the bigger the number of strange faces the less likelihood of receiving any worthwhile information. Strange accents are no asset either and the superintendant, the two inspectors and the four detectives might as well not be here at all. All they will succeed in doing by their continued presence is to frighten the wits out of the local population and even make these good people wary of myself since they will have no choice but to identify me with these intruders. I know they are well-trained and highly proficient in every respect but with all due respect what you require here are district men only led by yourself or you could bring in men like Jim Brick of Derrymullane and other outlying stations, men who know the people and the countryside and who are known and trusted by the people. With the brass out of the way the tip-offs will come. The locals will be making their own seemingly innocent enquiries here and there and a picture will emerge in time. The normal pattern of life has been disturbed and from the looks of things there will be more turbulance. A concensus of local opinion would tell you that no useful purpose will be served by the presence of so many strangers. They honestly feel that they're being made a show of. Consequently they close up. Any fair-minded person would agree that we should have been given first chance what with our knowledge of the area and the goodwill we have built up over the years. Fine then if we failed. Bring in the city men and give them their chance. I'll tell you a true story which will better illustrate what I am trying to prove. When I first came to this place more than thirty years ago I was looked upon as a stranger. It took several years before the people began to accept me as one of their own and even then there was the invisible barrier that always exists between the civic guard and the public but I knew all I wanted to know as soon as they came to accept me.

However, on my first day, while patrolling the village I was taught a valuable lesson. It was a fine summer's afternoon and there was nobody to be seen in the main street save an old, bearded man with a blackthorn stick. He sat on the wooden seat near the village pump. I bade him the time of day and stood idly for a few moments admiring the mountains of Mullachareirk in the hazy background. One stood out above the others and I was curious as to its name. I pointed in its general direction and asked the old man if he would tell me. He looked first at the peak and then he looked at me:

'I am here,' said he, 'man and boy for seventy-five years and I never noticed that mountain till now.'

I got the message and knew it would take time and patience if I were to win the confidence of these people. Do what you can Joe. We will never know who killed John and Sheila Glenn unless the investigation is in our hands. This is purely personal.

As ever,
Leo.

Dear Guard Molair:

It is with extreme regret I take up my pen to write to you. I have just come from the church where I have spent the past hour in prayer and meditation and beseeching the Mother of God to intercede for me and to guide my conscience in the right direction. It is my bounden duty to write this letter and inform you that the hit and run monster was in Fie's public house on the night the Glenns were slaughtered. He was in conversation most of the night with Margie Fie, the mistress of the den. It could be bad whiskey he got that blinded him when he went behind the wheel. Don't spare her. Act now.

> Devoted wife
> and mother of a large family.

Dear Guard Molair:

It is high time that someone in authority clamped down on the after-hours drinking that goes on at Crutt's shebeen which is the right name for it, may God forgive me. Everyone is saying that more drunken drivers leave it after hours than you would find coming from the city of Cork after a Munster final. Everybody says it must be in Crutt's the man responsible for this hit and run got the drink. Where there is smoke there is fire. Everybody says it and everybody can't be wrong and to see the Crutt one marching up the main aisle of the chapel like she was God's anointed. It would turn you against religion. Indeed it would and wouldn't you be inclined to ask yourself what is the good in being honest when the likes of her can scorn the laws of God and man and walk around brazen like she was a pure as the driven snow. Hell is a light punishment for the proprietors of

Crutt's public house.

Signed,
Indignant housewife.

Toormane Hill,
Monasterbawn.

Guard Molair:

The chickens have come home to roost. You have reaped the harvest of the shut eye and the turned back. On your shoulders fair and square must be placed the blame for the deaths of poor Mr and Mrs Glenn. May the faces of their innocent children haunt you to your death-bed although you won't see any death-bed for it is you has the prime head for an axe and fine soft neck for a rope, you that condoned after-hours drinking and ignored the warnings I sent you. It's you who should stand trial but you won't you wretch. May your conscience, if you have one, pester you till your days run out and you go to face your God. Think about what you have done, your crime against those orphaned babes.

Signed,
A T.T.

Garda Barracks,
Monasterbawn.

My dear Ned:

No doubt you have by now read the whole sorry business in the papers. They did a fair enough job allowing for all the groundless speculation and interviewing of local fools. They must dress things up too I suppose. I enclose a copy of my report plus a personal note to my chief Joe Fahy. You will also find a copy of the coroner's report. They may interest you. I had no written answer to the letter I wrote Joe Fahy. No blame to him for this. He came to see me, however, and we had a few drinks at the Widow's. There was nothing he could do. Mind you he agreed with most of my submission but he is himself subject to his own chief. He told me there is a prescribed machinery specially geared towards the crime in question and ready to move instantly into operation for the very good reason that scents grow cold and time covers most things. I asked him if there was any hope of just having the two local squad cars, their crews and all the men of our district alone just for a week but he ruled it out saying he had a moral obligation to accept all the help he could get and that he was under strict orders to follow routine and proven methods. My dear Ned I do not boast when I say I could do a better job than these outsiders, no blame to them, if I were given the manpower and transport and permitted to deploy it in my own way. But I'm only the man on the spot who know the people and the area better than any man in the entire force. They haven't asked for my advice once, just questioned me over and over like all the others involved in the case. They are stomping with big boots where tiptoe walking in soft shoes is absolutely necessary. They are closing doors instead of opening them.

The super also told me that the nationwide publicity was an advantage. The photograph of the six children in particular which appeared in two Sunday newspapers should bring home to those who might know something the fact that the perpetrator of the dastardly act must not be allowed to go free. The photos should prick consciences. They should but will they? Somewhere in the Monasterbawn district I'm sure, a mother or a father or a sister or brother or a whole family knows that one of its members is responsible for the taking of two lives yet nothing will induce them to talk. If young folk were responsible the parents know and vice versa. You're up against native craft and cunning here. Ordinary police methods won't work. I'll keep you posted about events. Quite frankly I'm pessimistic. In an area like Monasterbawn when solutions don't surface at once they have a habit of never surfacing. Love to all.

Your fond uncle,
Leo.

The Mountain Road,
Monasterbawn.

Dear Guard Molair:

You can pretend you was never in receipt of this. I would not care to be known as a man as writes to guards. I would like to see you. Slip up this way after dark and I'll have something for you, something will do you good although I owes you bugger-all after the persecution you gave me. Come on your lonesome and tell no one.

Thade Buckley,

P. S. That bull that gave you the run did the job himself crossing a gate. He got held up by a noose of thorny wire and hadn't the patience to wait. Don't come if there's a moon. I don't want the country seeing you.

Thade Buckley again.

P. S. I always lets on I'm illiterate so no one is going to believe you anyway if you say 'twas me wrote this letter. It pays me better to be illiterate.

T. B.

P. S. Don't come in a car whatever you do. Better you didn't come in uniform. Better you came in a hat and coat and I can say 'twas some chap enquiring after the services of my stud greyhound, Flashing Dango.

Yours fatefully,
T. B.

Dear Joe:

This is confidential. I was right all along. The brass have really put their feet in it. Yesterday I received a garbled message from a Mr Thade Buckley of the Mountain Road. He farms his mountain acres about five miles from the village. I deduced from the message that he knew something about the hit and run. I waited till well after dark and cycled to my rendezvous. There was no light in Thade Buckley's but this did not surprise me as I knew he wanted our meeting to be as secret as possible. The moment I dismounted he emerged from behind a hayrick and thrust a bottle into my hand.

'That's for yourself,' he said. 'Something to tickle the balls of your toes.'

It was a bottle of poitcheen, the last thing in the world I wanted.

'Is this why you told me to come up here?' I asked him.

''Tis a good drop,' he said, 'a special drop, the last of a good brew. When I got it you were the first man I thought of.'

I nearly went berserk at this. It gave me all I could do not to strike him. I took him by the throat and brought him to his knees.

'I'll beat you to pulp,' I told him, 'if you don't tell me the real reason why you invited me.'

'I don't know what you're talking about,' he whined. 'I swear it.'

'Come on, come on,' I said bringing him to his feet and chucking him about till he was dizzy. He still maintained, however, that his reason for inviting me was the poitcheen and the poitcheen alone. I tried different methods. I released him and offered him a cigarette.

'Tell me about the hit and run,' I asked him offhandedly.

'Hit and run,' he laughed at this. 'Cripes 'n mighty man,'

64

said he, 'I gave the morning long on that one with them detectives and that superintendent with the moustache. The morning long I gave and they quizzing me left and right, together and single.'

I knew that any further interrogation would be a waste of time, that the barriers were up. He had intended telling me something, knowing I wouldn't disclose my source. He knew he could trust me on that score. He knew from experience that I was a man who could be relied upon but the visit that morning from the detectives and the super had silenced him effectively and eternally. Nothing on God's earth would now induce him to part with his secret. I have my own suspicions but no proof at all. I'll report everything.

As ever,
Leo.

Fallon Street, G. S.,
Dublin 13.

Dear Leo:
My old friend. It's high time I wrote to you. I often have a good laugh when I remember the old days. Last Sunday I earned twenty-five pounds overtime. What a change. I often worked a long, hard and dirty month for the same amount not all that long ago. Your nephew is a fine lad, a bit over-conscientious on occasion but settling in nicely and will, no doubt, be a credit to the force in a short while now. I have a keen interest in him. By the way I'm a grandfather. My oldest daughter has a boy and a girl and my son has a son and heir with four months. I'm as bald now as a billiard ball, me that had a head of hair that blinded the women of Mayo, all but one and she, I'm told, died in England a short while ago.

That's a dirty business that hit and run you have. Without a tip-off you have little chance. At least that has always been my experience. The parents, of course, are the really guilty ones. They know damn well when something's wrong, particularly the mothers. Sometimes both parents know but mostly it's the mother and she hides it from the father unless the damage to the car is too obvious. Almost every hit and run would be solved overnight if parents made a brief examination of the son's car the morning after when a hit and run has taken place locally. Most of them prefer to close their eyes. This is also particularly true of wives whose husbands spend most nights in pubs and clubs. Theirs is a difficult choice but they do the easy thing, cover their eyes when they don't want to know, cover their mouths when they do know. In the short term it must seem to pay but in the long term the awful secret, too late now to be revealed, eats away at the mind like a vicious cancer. I wish you luck in your investigations. Drop me a line when the whole thing is over.

> Your old sidekick,
> Mick Drea.

P. S. We have lost the city streets to hooligans. The calibre of our men is as good as ever but physically we cannot hold a candle to the giants who dominated the city when I was a rookie. They would be suspended or dismissed altogether if they employed such tactics today. The spotlight nowadays is on the actions of the guards, never the hooligans. A low profile is what we are supposed to present. We must take every taunt and sometimes rough-handling. We must never retaliate. What many forget is that an effective police force cannot expect to be over-popular.

How many times lately have I wanted to smash my knuckles into the leering faces of cowardly scuts and blackguards, hell-bent on provoking me, you might say trained to the ounce in the art of provocation.

I bridle as any red-blooded man will bridle when I am taunted and teased, spat upon and cursed, called a pig and an animal and a free-state bastard whatever that means. I am challenged by drunkards and braggarts. I am called yellow, lily-livered, cowardly etc. I bridle but always I keep my temper and so we stay a step ahead of the lawbreaker.

Every job has its problems I have no doubt. Still ours is often unbearable. There are areas here where the inhabitants would cheerfully kick you to death for no reason at all. The uniform is enough. There is nothing from the general public by way of support. I often wish there were posses or vigilantes. Then the public might have some idea of what we have to contend with. But you have enough on your plate without my side of it. Drop a line sometime.

Mick.

Garda Barracks,
Monasterbawn.

Dear Mick:

Your letter brought back memories of old times. The past came drifting back to me again and I found myself walking along the narrow roads of Mayo like as if 'twas yesterday. Do you remember all the girls without lights on their cycles we used to stop at night after the dances? Fair play to us we never gave one a summons. You were the fierce man Drea for the cautioning so you were. Do you remember all the good-looking ones we escorted home for their own good moryah? Do you remember the lassie with the red hair that stole my cap? I called to her house a few days later by the way to find out how many hens, cows, ducks, pigs etcetera they had. The father gave me the numbers in good heart and we sat down to the tea.

'Will you also put it down in your returns,' said he, 'that I have four marriageable daughters and every one of them with a head redder than the next.'

We had a gay evening and my cap was returned to me before I left. Hard to believe but not one of those lovely girls was alive when I called that way again during a holiday four years later. All had been carried off by consumption.

I'm happy here Mick or at least I was happy until this hit and run. There isn't a day but we have a visit from some detective. They watch the comings and goings of the villagers and the pubs are losing trade steadily for no man wishes to have his movements recorded no matter how innocent or lawabiding he may be. The village was depressed enough after the accident but this constant harrassment is as much as it can take. They even have nicknames on the visitors now. One is called 'Catsfoot' because no one ever hears him approach. There is another and they call him 'The Pale Moonlight'. His first question is always: 'Who were you with last night?' There is another sinister looking chap, an inspector, who has a habit of scratching his posterior. 'Itchybum' they call him. Then there's 'The Big Wind' who breaks wind all the time and finally there is a giant of a fellow who walks like a lady. 'Tiptoe through the Tulips' they call him.

They see to it that the pubs close on the dot. With characteristic loyalty the regulars of Crutt's and Fie's are gradually drifting away to other pubs in the nearby villages. I had the usual anonymous letters from Crutt's and Fie's, both without a word of truth but they had to be handed over. The visitors took them seriously and acted accordingly. They questioned every man, woman and child who was seen entering or leaving either pub. It would take a brave man to go into one of them now. This whole business has me in the dumps. The respect I've earned over thirty years is being eroded. If only we could solve it things would soon return to normal.

I think I know who's responsible for this business myself. I'm keeping my own counsel just yet. There's little to go on. Mocky Trembles of Jackass Lane says he heard a loud thump around the time the accident would have taken place. Then he says he heard a car start and leave the scene for the direction of the Mountain Road. He was beating the wife when I called to see him. I intervened and gave him a good kick where it won't show.

'You'll kill her one of those days,' I warned him.

'There's no fear of that,' said Mocky, 'don't I know to the stroke what she can take.' Goggles Finn says he heard a car pass at the time but he never turned to look. He was too busy watching Aggie Boucher as she togged off for bed. Aggie herself saw the car pass but could give no clue otherwise. Aggie had a fellow up one time for carnal knowledge. She was dating a middle-aged mechanic from Mallow and in her own words in court he often started her engine. The mechanic had a son who was a total failure with women so what did he do but give the son his own coat, hat and spectacles and sent him off one dark and stormy night to meet Aggie at their favourite trysting place which was a hayshed convenient to Monasterbawn. The mechanic was a man of few words who always got down to business as soon as he arrived on the scene. Aggie did most of the talking asking how was this and how was that and never waiting for an answer only always pressing on to the next question or commenting at length on the state of the country in general and the state of Monasterbawn in particular. She took the mechanic's actions for granted, making no comment during the preparatory stages of the encounter, during the act itself or afterwards. There are apparently many women who behave like this in these circumstances and Aggie Boucher was one of them.

The son had been carefully briefed by the father and he carried out his instructions to the letter. It was a big moment for him since there was no other way he could possibly come to close quarters with a woman. For a while all went well. The preliminary stages were negotiated successfully and the heart rose in the son of the mechanic after this first hurdle was cleared. Gently then he laid her on the broad of her back on the hay. With a becoming sigh just like the father he got directly down to business. It was a task to his liking and he lay into it with a will, with too much of a will alas for suddenly Aggie Boucher pulled out from under him and started to screech like a stuck pig. She reported the incident to the barracks and identified the son of the mechanic. It should never have gone to court but it did. The son denied the charge and the father backed him up by insisting that he was Aggie's lover on the night in question. Aggie stuck to her guns. She was asked by the judge how she could be sure it was the son in the darkness of the shed.

'I knew at once,' said she, 'for there is no one has the fine even stroke of the father.' The judge who himself was a middle-aged man held in her favour.

To get back to the hit and run Aggie saw the car but no more could she tell and it is highly unlikely that she would tell if she saw more. Thade Buckley obviously saw the car too but he has been frightened off and there is nothing to be done with him. About a mile from Thade's there is a farm owned by Malachy Rattin. He has a wife, three sons and four daughters. They have an ancient Austin and a tractor but neither was involved in the accident. I'm sure about this. I thoroughly checked both vehicles unknown to them while they were drinking in Monasterbawn. The Rattin girls are sonsy types who spread their favours widely although I am told that the oldest girl has a steady man. If he has a car he could have driven her home on the night of the hit and run. I was up there yesterday on my own. They offered me tea which accepted. I told them I was looking for information and then went on to explain that if there was a passenger in the car which was involved that person would most certainly escape scot free if he or she came forward and made a statement to the guards. I thought I detected a twitch on the face of the girl who had served the tea but oul' Rattin intervened immediately.

'Yesterday,' said he, '"The Big Wind" and "Tiptoe Through the Tulips" were here. "Tiptoe" drank out of that very cup in your hand. We told them all we knew which was damn-all. We answered every question they put to us. It

70

would be a great ease to us now if we was left alone and not have the neighbours raising all sorts of talk over guards coming two days in a row.'

I apologised for any embarrassment I might be causing and expressed a desire to speak to the girl alone. The father was inclined to object but when I asked if she had anything to hide he agreed. I led the girl out into the roadway out of earshot of the father or any other who might be listening. 'You're the eldest girl,' I said to her. She nodded demurely.

'And you're doing a strong line I hear.' Again the demure nod. Too demure to be true.

'Tell me,' said I, 'what part of the world does your young man hail from?'

'Tooreenfada,' she answered.

'That would be the best part of twenty miles from here?' I said.

''Tis no secret where it is,' said she as demure as ever, 'isn't it carried on the signposts.'

I was dealing with a tough chicken, well drilled by the Da and well used all her life to dealing with curious strangers. It wasn't my first time calling to the Rattin household. I could put forty minor crimes at their door but I could never prove one. They were always on the one word every one of them, produced and rehearsed by the Da with never an extra line or part of a line no matter how often you questioned them.

'Tell me Miss Rattin,' said I, 'what is your young man's name?'

'His name,' said she, ''is McMorrow, Joseph McMorrow. They calls him Sikey.'

'And was Sikey at the dance,' I enquired, 'the night of the hit and run?'

'He comes every Sunday night,' she answered demurely, 'but sure didn't I tell all this to "Big Wind" and "Tiptoe" and before that to "Catsfoot" and "Itchybum".'

'Sure if you told it to them you can have no objection in telling it to me.'

'My Da is your sound man,' said she.

'How come?' I asked.

'He says that there's no good to be got o' guards.'

'Now Miss Rattin,' said I, 'was your young man driving a car the night of the hit and run?'

'No.'

'And how did he come to the dance?'

'With his brother.' She started to tap her foot impatiently. She drew a cigarette butt and a box of matches from the sleeve of her cardigan and soon she was puffing away in full content. Something told me that she knew more than she was disclosing. She was nervous and worried and she did not altogether conceal this successfully. I tried another tack.

'Had Sikey ever a car?' I asked.

'He had but he sold it three months ago.'

'Does he ever hire out a self-drive?'

'No he don't.'

'Does he ever borrow a car?'

'I don't know.'

'Since he sold his own car did he ever come driving another car?'

'Once only,' said she, 'and that was two months ago.'

'And where did he get that car?'

'He borrowed it from a cousin I think but he was covered for wasn't he stopped the same night by the White Mice and let go at once.'

I thanked her and let her go. I noticed a peakishness about her and there was a decided swing to her walk. I was sure she was pregnant and had been for some time. If Sikey was the father it would be in the girl's best interests to keep her mouth shut. When I got back to the Barracks I compared notes with the inspector. He agreed when I suggested Sikey should be questioned. He promised to do the job himself. Said it was the best lead to date.

If you are ever in this neck of the woods be sure to call. I always keep a good drop. No man will be more welcome. We must continue to keep in touch now that we have started to correspond again. I intend to come out next year. Have you decided one way or the other yet?

All the best for now,
Sincerely,
Leo.

Derrymullane G. S.

Dear Leo:

I haven't time to drop over since the fellow here took queer. He was always bad but for the past few weeks he hasn't appeared much only talking to himself. I can hear him in the day-room. There's no more talk now of your hit and run. A nine day wonder that, add a few weeks. I was doing a bit of arithmetic lately and I discovered that there have been seven unsolved hit and run cases in this district in the past five years as against one solved and he gave himself up after a day. Family affairs, every one of them. I can hear your man at it upstairs. He had an uncle for a bishop. That's how he became a sergeant. That's as far as he got however. The real trouble with him is that he thinks he's a super. That's why he won't speak to me. He feels he'd be letting down his rank. Whenever I want him to sign something or confirm something I have to pretend I'm a super too. I go up and knock at the door and put on an English accent.

'Who's out?' he calls.

''Tis me,' I tell him, 'Superintendant McDoogle.'

'Come in, Come in,' he says. After that we get down to business and the affairs of the station are easily sorted out. Superintendant Fahy knows the score. His advice is to leave well alone unless the man becomes dangerous. Three times I knocked on the door yesterday and got no answer. Finally I had to pretend I was the commissioner. All was well after that. The other night he ordered me to sandbag the doors and windows saying he had word of an I.R.A.

73

attack. He mightn't be too far wrong the way things are going. Sooner or later the banks and post-offices of our own district will come under attack. It's happening elsewhere. Why shouldn't it happen here? Whisht. Here he comes. He had just ordered me to suspend every civic guard in the station for disrespect to the superintendent. He keeps forgetting there's only the two of us here. It can't go on. Almost every day now he has visitors to his upstairs room. Sometimes he tells me who they are and why they came. Other times he cannot say a word for security reasons. On Thursday he had a call from Princess Grace of Monaco. Apparently she wanted him to take charge of the police force there. Later that day there was a deputation from Saudi Arabia. He introduced me to these. One of them was a very nice man by the name of Haji Puree. The others were a dour lot. That night a superintendent from Scotland Yard called to pay his respects. He was on a fishing holiday. He told him if we ever decided to leave the guards the Yard will be delighted to have us. Our man already works for them and for the F.B.I. and Interpol in a consultative capacity. This morning there was a lot of noise upstairs, an attempt on his life by some Chinese agitators. He managed to beat them off.

What am I going to do? I can't give up on him. Last Sunday I spent the whole day on checkpoint duty. When I came back that night he told me that he had made an important arrest. Apparently there had been a papal spy in the area for some weeks. For some reason known only to the Pope she had been watching the comings and goings at the barracks in Derrymullane. At first I thought he was up to his usual capers but then I heard a dull thump from the area where the cell is located.

'Be careful,' he cautioned.

'I will. I will,' I promised. 'I'll just have a look.'

'There's no point,' he said angrily, 'she hasn't a word of English.'

'I'll take a look anyway,' I told him.

74

'It's against regulations,' he warned and moved to stop me.

'Did she say anything?' I asked.

'The usual,' he replied.

'What was that?' I asked.

'She pleaded diplomatic immunity.'

Meanwhile there were several thumps and some other unidentifiable, muffled sounds from the direction of the cell. He had by now unloosened his tunic and drawn his baton.

'I have a duty,' he said proudly, 'and no power on earth can dissuade me from carrying out that same.'

'What's that noise upstairs?' I said.

'What noise?' he asked suspiciously.

'Italian voices,' I said.

He was upstairs like a flash and there was pandemonium above. I'm telling you the furniture paid for it. I hastened to the cell while he was out of the way and there bound and gagged was Mrs Hussey the char. She was in a shocked state but fair play to her the first question she asked was to find out if himself was alright. She must have known with a while but kept her own counsel. There are more of them that would have us noted. I sent her home. She assured me that no one would hear a word from her. The commotion upstairs had ended and he was coming down the stairs with several dangerous-looking Italians in tow. One had a scar and another a limp. They were a terrible assortment of cut-throats. We managed to lock them up. He said nothing about Mrs Hussey. At the back of his mind somewhere he knew he had done wrong. He was right now however. He had the real villians under lock and key.

We took their names but every man Jack of them pleaded diplomatic immunity and swore like troopers at us. Christ I'm beginning to be as bad as him. It can't be too long now before he cracks. I'll let you know. He'll have to be moved quietly. Have you really made up your mind about coming out? I couldn't afford it just yet. The kids are too young awhile.

As always,
Jim Brick.

Garda Barracks,
Monasterbawn.

Dear Ned:

I hope yourself, herself and the ladeen are fine. The story
here could be worse I daresay. We are disappointed naturally
over the hit and run. All our visitors have gone and so alas
have the children of the dead pair. They've gone to a good
place, run by sisters. Before he left the inspector told me
about his interview with the prime suspect, a chap we'll call
Sikey. Mick Drea will have filled you in on the story so far.
I told him all in my last letter. This fellow Sikey is from a
place called Tooreenfada about twenty miles away. He is
doing a strong line with a young one called Rattin from the
Mountain Road. The inspector who was christened 'Itchybum' by the locals is a tenacious enough fellow, highly
intelligent but with a downright bad manner which has
antagonised everybody. There is no doubt in his mind, or in
mine, that Sikey was the driver of the car which killed John
and Sheila Glenn. He was in town that night. He did drive
the Rattin girl home. He was seen by at least two locals
who will never come forward. The car was one of twenty
crocks owned by a cousin of his with a run-down garage. It
had been in a crash but so had every other car in the
cousin's lot. Sikey's brothers, three of them, his cousin and
all the Rattin girls will swear that Sikey had no car of his
own on the night of the hit and run. Sikey is to marry the
Rattin girl at the end of this month. A friend of the Widow
Hansel's told her that there would be a baby less than a
month afterwards. Those who know that Sikey killed the
Glenns can salve their consciences by telling themselves that
the young mother and child would be the real victims if

their evidence was the cause of convicting him. All the Rattins know, all Sikey's people and at least two others know but the Gardai know nothing. It's sickening. There may be more who know but you may be sure they'll never talk.

There are certain elements in every community who have always obstructed or conspired against the guards, who have closed ranks and stood firm when one or more of them was accused or suspected of something. It is a feather in their caps when we fail to right a wrong or punish a transgression and by God they show it in their faces when we accost them in the streets after a victory. There is the provocative, knowing smile that every one of us knows so well.

This is the eighth serious hit and run in this district in five years. There have been five deaths and four maimings and there is nothing to show that it won't get worse. The mothers know and the wives know and sometimes the fathers and other members of the family know. There are cases where the neighbours know. In all there must be a hundred people who could help us solve these killings and maimings but not one single, solitary voice has emerged so far from this community of so-called, law-abiding people. They all know but us. That's the way it's always been and unless the make-up of mankind changes that's the way it always will be. If that's the sort of law they want that's the sort of law they deserve.

Thade Buckley's stud greyhound Flashing Dango was also killed the other night by a driver who did not stop. I thought this might soften him but so far he has remained silent. That was the mourning after the death of the dog. They have been drowning their sorrows in Crutt's and Fie's for the past three nights but always leaving on the dot of closing time and never unsteady on their feet or showing the least sign of drink. When they see me patrolling they whisper among themselves and there is the faintest trace of derisive laughter. I march on and keep my feelings to myself. The wheel turns slowly but turn it does and some day it will stop at the right number or at least I hope it will. Take good care of yourself up there and good care of herself and the kid as well. Now that I plan to retire you'll probably see a good deal of me from time to time but that's a fair ways off yet and the future is in God's good hands. I had better sign off. I'm up to my eyes between passports, school attendances, dog licenses and noxious weeds and on top of that a report that Mocky Trembles has the wife murdered. This must be the hundredth time. There's a complaint from a mother that her seventeen year old son has been served with cider at Fie's and is currently out of his mind. Jamesy Cracken, all seventy-four years of him, has just now attempted to rape the daily help. Monica Flynn has reported the Bugger Moran. That particular naughty boy has been exposing himself again. Goggles Finn has been peeping in the wrong windows. If only he would confine himself to Aggie Boucher's all would be well. Last night he spent an hour trying to watch the postmistress undressing herself. Will the long shameful, pitiful parade never end or is there any way in the world's face to divert it. I think I'll call on Jerry Fogg and take a saunter in the general direction of the Widow's, have a game of cards maybe with a few of the boys and down a few pints. God knows I have them well earned this day. Write soon.

Your fond uncle,
Leo.

Fallon Street, G. S.
Dublin 13.

Dear Uncle Leo:

Enjoyed your letter. You never know but a break may come in that hit and run case when you least expect it. It can be terribly frustrating when the public won't come forward. They foolishly believe that it's the function of the gardai and the guards alone to solve crimes but a police force is only as strong as the moral fibre of the public it represents and what the public really wants is not to be bothered in any way or embarrassed by the publicity the courts can bring or drawn into things against their will. The public would like to see us winning the war against crime. I have no doubt about that. However, they would like to keep their eyes shut while we are engaged in the struggle.

The reason I am writing so soon is that I am off to the Border for a term of duty. Herself and the kid are off to the mother-in-law until I come back. It's my second term so I know what to expect. You'll be hearing from me.

Your fond nephew,
Ned.

Monasterbawn G. S.

Dear Mick:

You remember our friend Jim Brick? Well he's been stationed next door in Derrymullane for years now with a sergeant who thinks he's a superintendent. God alone knows what he has suffered in silence for the good name of the force. At last his suffering has come to an end. On Wednesday night last I received a phone-call from Jim saying that his man had become violent and was barricaded in a room upstairs. It would be two hours before a squad car became available because of a bank robbery in the village of Tooreenfada. I had no choice but to contact Jack Fie the publican who is a tight-lipped fellow and has a car. Fie's wife is a sharp-tongued dangerous gossip but the man himself is a decent sort who never has a bad word to say about anyone. Although hen-pecked to the limits of his endurance he is an agreeable and obliging man. When I asked him to drive me to Derrymullane he agreed at once and we set out in a blinding rainstorm for that place. When we arrived there was no change in the situation. Jim met me at the door. I introduced Fie and the three of us made our way indoors. We decided our best bet would be to transport him to headquarters where the Garda doctor would be available. At all costs Jim wanted no commotion. His sole aim was to get the poor man out of Derrymullane without attracting attention. With this in view we sent Jack Fie upstairs with the following instructions. He was to knock upon the door and inform the sergeant that he was to come at once to meet the Minister for Justice who was waiting for him in Mallow and that a staff car was available to transport him thence.

Jim and I waited at the foot of the stairs. Jim had a pair of handcuffs at the ready. Upstairs we heard the door open and heard Jack Fie's voice.

'This way sir,' he said and indicated the way downstairs. They came slowly, the sergeant first, Jack Fie second. They exchanged remarks about the weather. At the foot of the stairs the sergeant stopped. Jim and I saluted and prayed silently that there would be no trouble. Suddenly the sergeant turned and struck Jack Fie a solid blow on the jaw. Fie fell in a heap at the foot of the stairs. I tackled the sergeant down low by his ankles while Jim endeavoured to get the handcuffs on. The man had superhuman strength. All we could do was to hold on to him until he weakened or we did. Suddenly he went limp and started to weep. Then he spoke rationally.

'It's alright Jim,' he said, 'there's no need for the bracelet.'

Then as sane as ever I saw a man he got up and went straight to the car. He sat in the back without a further word.

The most recent reports indicate that he has a good chance of returning to normalcy although he will never return to the force. The basic reason for his condition, according to those who knew him, was the fact that he had been by-passed for promotion several times while colleagues of his with less experience and ability were pulled up over his head. As the years went by he began to stagnate in

Derrymullane with no outlet for his talents. A normal man might make the most of it or just go to seed as many good men did but not our friend. A new sergeant arrived yesterday in Derrymullane, a spick and span merchant, something of a martinet. The barracks of Derrymullane won't be long knocking the taspy out of him. Better still a couple of chip shop rows and a few weeks on checkpoint duty when the wind is from the north with sleet in it and you'd be ashamed to let a dog out of doors. I'll close for now hoping to hear from you at your convenience.

> Take good care,
> Your old pal,
> Leo.

Monasterbawn G. S.

Dear Joe:

At the moment things look black but I have great hopes that someone somewhere will talk when the dust settles. I have just received another letter from Thade Buckley but I haven't opened it yet. If there was a blue riband for the ripest rogue in Monasterbawn Thade would win hands down. He had his share of misfortune too. His oldest boy was killed about ten years ago in a fall from his motorbike. Inevitable since he never wore a helmet. Today whenever I see a young man without a helmet on a fast machine I feel like cursing the parents who saw him leave home without suitable headgear.

The first time I prosecuted Thade was for the larceny of a pair of shoes. It was old Dan Turndown's wake. He was laid out in his best for all to see in his son's house on Toormane Hill. All night the neighbours called to pay their respects. They praised the corpse, accepted a drink and sat for a while in the kitchen.

It was well into the morning of another day when Thade arrived. He went straight to the wake-room to say a prayer for the soul of Dan Turndown. When he returned to the

81

kitchen he declined the offer of a drink on the gounds that he had a cow calving.

A little after daybreak the woman of the house rose from her bed. The first thing she did was to visit the wake-room with a view to tidying up. It was she who noticed the torn wellingtons on the feet of the corpse. It was a month later, at a wren dance in Toormane, that I caught Thade Buckley dancing an eight-hand reel in Dan Turndown's new shoes.

Still I had better read the letter. I'll be in touch.

As ever,
Leo.

The Mountain Road,
Monasterbawn.

Dear Guard Molair:
Sunday night will be quiet here with all gone to pubs and dances saving myself and my missus who has too much sense for that sort of thing no more. Nine o'clock would be fine time to meet under the lone eye of Ballygownalawn Bridge where no one will see or hear saving what few fish there is in the hole down below. This time I'll have some-thing that will warm the cockles of your heart and no codding. No poitcheen this time but a thing you would dearly love to know.

There is wretches loose in this countryside that should be dangling from the gallows, and their seed and breed should be strung up with them and their corpses left out-side the gate of churches so as honest people know what they have done. Is it people I ask you that would harm innocent creatures? Is it hounds that would take the life of an innocent dog that brought credit and renown to Monasterbawn and the nation? Be here Sunday night at nine and tell no one. It is no good for you to go to supers or the likes with this as I am illiterate and can get several

to swear to that effect. Remember Ballygownalawn Bridge
at nine o'clock on your lonesome.

Signed,
Thade Buckley.

P. S. The bull you prosecuted me for I took to Derrymullane Mart. He was not a full bull since he got himself
perverted by the thorny wire I told you about. He is what
they call a Dildo. He could perform alright but no good
would come of it. The man I sold him to has no way of
knowing this but all is fair in love and war as we learned in
school long ago.

T. B.

P. S. In the name of God let you not wear a uniform in
case someone might see me going up and you going down.
If you should come across anyone on the road that knows
you let on you're looking for bald tyres. In this country
there is a fierce crop of these as you know yourself and if
you were to summons them all you would bankrupt the
parish of Monasterbawn.

T. B.

P. S. What I have to tell you will put your mind at ease for
once and for all concerning a certain item that has caused a
deal of commotion in these parts lately.

*　　　*　　　*

When Leo Molair came down from the mountain he was
elated as Moses was elated after God had entrusted him
with the Commandments. Although the information which
Thade Buckley had imparted to him was not nearly so
important as God's revelation to Moses it was, nevertheless,

83

priceless in its own context. Infuriated by the untimely demise of his dearly beloved greyhound, Flashing Dango, Thade had unflinchingly put the finger on the man responsible for the deaths of John and Sheila Glenn. It was, as Leo and 'Itchybum' had surmised, Sikey from Tooreenfada. Thade himself had not seen the actual incident but his youngest daughter had. She had immediately informed Thade who responded by threatening to break her neck if ever she mentioned a word to anybody. She had also seen another witness, Goggles Finn, who promptly ran off as soon as the victims were smashed to the ground.

Later when Leo confronted him with this he admitted everything and identified Sikey of Tooreenfada as the driver of the car. Sikey's companion at the time was the Rattin girl who carried his child. After the crash he left the car, made a brief inspection of the bodies and drove off.

Leo was commended by his superintendent Joe Fahy who assured him that the evidence against Sikey was so overwhelming that there was no way he could escape prison.

So life went on. Time passed and came the last summer of Leo Molair's life as custodian of the peace for Monasterbawn. He looked forward to his retirement and engaged a builder from Derrymullane to erect a bungalow on the plot he had long before purchased for such a purpose. He was on his way to Derrymullane to meet this man when the unexpected caught up with him.

Some said later that since he was out of uniform it was none of his business but most held that being the man he was no other course was open to him. At precisely ten o'clock he left Monasterbawn barracks and mounted his bicycle. At one minute past ten he cycled past Monasterbawn post office. He got no further. Seated in a car parked directly outside the building was a young man who was known to him as a subversive. He had once seen him during an anti-government demonstration in the city. As Leo was about to pass by the man tried to cover off his profile with his hands. It was too late. Leo had recognised him. At once he linked the man's presence with the fact that it was family allowance day and that a substantial amount of cash would be in the post office. Leo dismounted and, as he did, a number of things happened.

*   *   *

Main Street,
Monasterbawn.

Dear Ned:

It's high time I dropped you a line. At the funeral I couldn't help but notice your resemblance to himself. You asked me to send you a personal account of what happened. At a minute past ten on that awful morning a man entered Monasterbawn post office waving a gun and demanding that all the money on the premises be turned over to him. I was in the office at the time with Mrs Dully the Postmistress. She handed over the money which amounted to six hundred and ten pounds. The man ran into the street still waving a gun just as your Uncle Leo was entering the post office. He seized the robber by both hands and disarmed him. I was standing just inside the window at the time but my feet were stuck to the floor. I was paralysed by shock. The robber's accomplice who happened to be sitting in a car parked outside lowered the window and pointed a gun at your uncle. He fired two shots. The first struck Leo in the chest but did not seem to take immediate effect. The second struck him in the forehead. He fell dead at once. The two men drove off. Nobody knows who they were or where they came from. All we know is that they murdered the finest gentleman ever to come into our midst and left a void that will remain through my time and yours and beyond. There's no more I can say except that I'll tend to his grave as if he was my own father till I'm taken away myself for, in truth, that is what he was, a father to me and mine and to every man, woman and child in his care.

Yours faithfully,
Jerry Fogg.

THE END

LETTERS OF AN IRISH PUBLICAN

In this book we get a complete picture of life in Knockanee as seen through the eyes of a publican, Martin MacMeer. He relates his story to his friend Dan Stack who is a journalist. He records in a frank and factual way events like the cattle fair where the people 'came in from the hinterland with caps and ash-plants and long coats', and the cattle stood 'outside the doors of the houses in the public streets'. Through his remarkable perception we 'get a tooth' for all the different characters whom he portrays with sympathy, understanding and wit. We are overwhelmed by the charms of the place where at times 'trivial incidents assume new proportions.' These incidents are exciting, gripping, hilarious, touching and uncomfortable.

THE GENTLE ART OF MATCHMAKING
and other important things

This book offers a feast of Keane, one of Ireland's best loved playwrights. The title essay reminds us that while some marriages are proverbially made in heaven, others have been made in the back parlour of a celebrated pub in Listowel and none the worse for that! But John B. Keane has other interests besides matchmaking, and these pieces mirror many moods and attitudes. Who could ignore Keane on Potato-Cakes? Keane on skinless sausages? or Half-Doors? Is there a husband alive who will not recognise someone near and dear to him when he reads, with a mixture of affection and horror, the essay 'Female Painters'? And, more seriously, there are other pieces that reflect this writer's deep love of tradition: his nostalgic re-creation of an Irish way of life that is gone forever.

SELF PORTRAIT

John B. Keane's own story has all the humour and insight
one would expect, but it has too, the feeling of an Irish
countryman for his traditional way of life and his ideas
for the Ireland he loves.

PLAYS

THE FIELD
THE MAN FROM CLARE
BIG MAGGIE
THE YEAR OF THE HIKER
MOLL
THE CHANGE IN MAME FADDEN
VALUES
THE CRAZY WALL

LOVE POEMS OF THE IRISH
Edited by Sean Lucy

This anthology shows those people who seem to think that
we are a loveless race, how wrong they are. It takes a wide
view of what can be called love poetry, a view which embraces
a whole landscape of feeling between men and women as men
and women, and does not confine itself to poems about being
'in love' in the more restricted meaning of that term.

THE TAILOR AND ANSTY
Eric Cross

The tailor and his wife lived in Co Cork, yet the width of the
world could barely contain his wealth of humour and fantasy.
Marriages, inquests, matchmaking — everything is here.

THE FARM BY LOUGH GUR
Mary Carbery

This is the true story of a family who lived on a farm by
Lough Gur, the Enchanted Lake, in Co Limerick. Their
home, shut away from the turmoil of politics, secure from
apprehension of unemployment and want, was a world in
itself. The master with his men, the mistress with her
maids worked in happy unity. The four little girls,
growing up in this contented atmosphere, dreamed of
saints and fairies. The story is also a picture of manners
and customs in a place so remote that religion had still
to reckon with pagan survivals, where a fairy-doctor
cured the landlord's bewitched cows, and a banshee
comforted the dying with the music of harps and flutes.

THE BOOK OF IRISH CURSES
Patrick C. Power

A remarkable blend of history, folklore and anecdote, this is above all a book about people and about cursing as an ancient and mysterious agency of their fears and hatreds.

THE PERMISSIVE SOCIETY IN IRELAND?
Emer O'Kelly

This book in which case histories are given in the form of interviews makes interesting reading and perhaps it will help us to understand why people opt out of our society, sometimes through no fault of their own.

THE SEXUAL CHRISTIAN
Urban G. Steinmetz

Controversial, hard-hitting, yet at the same time, a sensitive exploration of what it means to be sexual and christian. Urban Steinmetz gets down from what he calls his sexual rubbish dump in search of an upretending Christianity.

IRISH MARRIAGE – HOW ARE YOU!
Nuala Fennell

This book presents in a powerful, evocative and graphic way the truth about many Irish marriages. The letters come from Nuala Fennell's own files and each tells a woman's story of what it is like to be trapped in the living hell which is an Irish marriage gone wrong.

I'M NOT AFRAID TO DIE
By an Irish Housewife

I'm Not Afraid to Die is the autobiography of an ordinary
suburban housewife. Over the years she has acquired a
husband, reared two children and built up a happy home.
On a sunny spring day her doctor, a life-long friend,
confirms her fears, she is to be another victim of the
modern day killer — cancer. The story starts with life
and a certain amount of bravado. Born at the bottom
of the stairs and reared in a cotton wool filled boot box
was not a very promising beginning. Being fed exclusively
on brandy and water with sugar, added a touch of luxury.
Things brightened up while she was farmed out to stay
with Tits Murphy in Co Cork. Tits put the whole world
into perspective with one indignant wag of her huge bosoms.

TOMORROW TO BE BRAVE
J. M. Feehan

This is the story of a brave woman's fight against cancer
and death. Mary Feehan was a remarkable and wonderful
woman who knew she was going to die a lingering and
painful death but who faced up to it with unbelievable
courage and who turned her last terrible years on this
earth into the greatest years of her life — years of kind-
ness, patience, understanding and unselfishness.

ARCHBISHOP MAGRATH
The Scoundrel of Cashel
Robert Wyse Jackson

Miler Magrath was appointed Bishop of Down and Connor by the Pope. Later he was invested by Queen Elizabeth I as Protestant Archbishop of Cashel and for a number of years successfully held both opposing positions and drew revenues from each Diocese.

In Irish eyes he has always been referred to as that 'wicked Archbishop, a notorious manipulator and trimmer, the man you love to hate'. And yet as Dr Jackson probes the character of Miler one cannot help feeling something like affection for him.

He lived for 100 years, and by so doing came near to spanning the gulf between the bloodthirsty world of medieval Ireland and the polished Anglo-Irish elite of Berkeley and Swift.

THE COURSE OF IRISH HISTORY
Edited by T. W. Moody and F. X. Martin

This is the first book of its kind—a rapid survey, with a geographical introduction, of the whole course of Ireland's history from the middle Stone Age to 1966, written by 21 scholars, all specialists in their own field.

THE ULSTER QUESTION 1603-1975
Prof. T. W. Moody

The aim of this book is to guide and help the ordinary person to understand the reasons, both past and present, for the bitter strife in Northern Ireland. It traces the historical significance of Ulster in the history of Ireland before and after the English conquest and since the plantation in the early seventeenth century, when the foundations of the modern British and Protestant colony were laid and the Protestant-Catholic polarisation that has characterised Ulster's society ever since began. It also seeks to explain the political instability of Northern Ireland in terms both of relations between Protestants and Catholics within the six counties and of relations between Northern Ireland, the Irish Republic and Britain.

IN IRELAND LONG AGO
Kevin Danaher

Those who have only the most hazy ideas about how our ancestors lived in Ireland will find enlightenment in these essays which range widely over the field of Irish folklife. Kevin Danaher describes life in Ireland before the 'brave new world' crept into the quiet countryside. Or perhaps 'describe' is not the right word. He rather invites the reader to call on the elderly people at their homes, to listen to their tales and gossip and taste their food and drink; to step outside and marvel at their pots and pans, ploughs and flails; to meet a water diviner; to join a faction fight; hurry to a wedding and bow down in remembrance of the dead.

Not only does the author write about people with reverence, but those people are reverently introduced to the reader by their own words, as whenthe Kerryman replied to the Dublin man who asked him if he could take a photograph of his donkey with the baskets: 'You never saw one before? Oh man, you must be from a very backward part of the country!' In this book Kevin Danaher has not only given us a well balanced picture of life in Ireland, but has also gone far to capture the magic of the written word.

FOLKTALES OF THE IRISH COUNTRYSIDE
Kevin Danaher

A delightful collection of tales simply told and suitable for the whole family.

IRISH COUNTRY PEOPLE
Kevin Danaher

Irish Country People is simply one fascinating glorious feast of folklore and interesting sidelights of history recorded without a fraction of a false note or a grain of sentimentality. The topics covered in the twenty essays range over a wide field of history, folklore, mythology and archaeology. There are discussions about cures, curses and charms; lords, labourers and wakes; names, games and ghosts; prayers and fairy-tales. Nowadays we find it hard to visualise the dark winter evenings of those times when there was no electric light, radio, television or cinemas. We find it harder to realise that such evenings were not usually long enough for the games, singing, card-playing, music, dancing and story-telling that went on.

We can read about a six-mile traffic jam near Tailteann in the year 1168, just before the Norman invasion, and the incident is authenticated by a reference to the *Annals of the Four Masters*. The whole book is tinged with quiet humour: 'You should always talk to a dog in a friendly, mannerly way, but you should never ask him a question directly, for what would you do if he answered you, as well he might?'

GENTLE PLACES AND SIMPLE THINGS
Kevin Danaher

If the four-leafed shamrock was lucky, the hungry grass was quite the opposite, and very unlucky indeed was he who trod on it. In point of fact, if you trod on the hungry grass you almost expired of hunger—for this was where some poor wretch died of starvation in the famine days. The hungry grass is still remembered in Ireland, like the stories of highwaymen, travelling people and Danaher chats about highwaymen, more or less noble robbers, of summer pastures, of the typical Irish 'Whiteboys', of lost and hidden treasures. He tells all sorts of tales about the beliefs associated with birds, insects and big and little animals, of plants, bushes, trees and stones. Then we hear about dwarfs and fabulous water monsters, and ghosts and witches, about castles and drowned cities.

Kevin Danaher's books are such that anyone, young or old, be he an enthusiast for folklife or not, can pick them up and derive pleasure and profit from reading them.

THE PLEASANT LAND OF IRELAND
Kevin Danaher

This book is well illustrated and gives a comprehensive picture of a way of life which though in great part is vanishing is still familiar to many of our countrymen.

Send us your name and address if you would like to receive our complete catalogue of books of Irish Interest

THE MERCIER PRESS
4 Bridge Street, Cork, Ireland